To Gail:

KEEPER OF THE GREEN FIRE

A Novel

By

Robert Edney

authorHOUSE®

AuthorHouse™
1663 Liberty Drive
Bloomington, IN 47403
www.authorhouse.com
Phone: 1-800-839-8640

First published by AuthorHouse 11/2/2010

ISBN: 978-1-4520-6182-5 (e)
ISBN: 978-1-4520-6181-8 (sc)
ISBN: 978-1-4520-6180-1 (hc)

Library of Congress Control Number: 2010912199

Printed in the United States of America

This book is printed on acid-free paper.

TABLE OF CONTENTS

ACKNOWLEDGEMENTS

I dedicate this book to the memory of my wife, Betty Gibbs Edney, my daughters, Particia Edney Doucette and Ann Edney Pyle.

Special thanks to Pamela S. Jones, MPH who corrected the typed the manuscript.

Elizabeth McCary Owen, a dear friend who constantly encouraged me.

For the memory of those Cherokee people who were shamefully up rooted from their homes in western North Carolina and forced to march in "The Trail of Tears" to Oklahoma.

FOREWORD

The setting for this story is centered in North Carolina, perhaps then it's only fitting to give a brief description of the state – it's remarkable geographic features and historical background, both of which her people are so richly blessed.

Being an eastern mid-Atlantic coastal state, it is sandwiched between Virginia on the north and Carolina to the south, Georgia and Tennessee flank it to the west. The state joins a few others that are unique, that is, it has three distinct different sections that differ, both geographically and dialect. For instance, if you were to talk to a mountain man, his manner of speech would be somewhat different than a native brought up near the coast.

Three main sections make up the state coastal plains, piedmont and mountains. The coastal plains start at the "outer banks" and extend westward, where it joins the piedmont plateau. If the water were from the mainland to the outer banks were included, it would represent about forty percent of the state.

Elevations of this section range from sea level up to one hundred feet where it butts against the fall line and piedmont plateau. This is a vast area of coniferous forest and large farms. Forest products and agriculture are the main industries here. Also, fishing and tourism are important to the economy.

The heartland or piedmont area is a vast array of small farms and huge manufacturing industries. The forest is a mixture of hardwoods and pine, which support the wood products industry. Elevations start at the fall line of around one hundred feet and end at the foot of the mountains, at twelve hundred feet.

The mountain section takes up only twenty percent of the state. Elevations start at twelve hundred feet and rise to over six thousand feet on the mountain peaks. Hardwood forests predominate, however, coniferous species, such as hemlock, white pine, red spruce and Frazer fir are also abundant.

Small farms, including apple orchards are numerous. The wood industry is important. Mining was once very important, but has gradually receded.

The state is covered by many rivers and streams, which start in the northwest and flow southeastward, where they drain into the Atlantic Ocean. Streams, west of the continental divide, flow southwest and empty into the Gulf of Mexico. Temperatures are generally mild in North Carolina. During the growing season they range from seventy-eight in the mountains to over ninety in the lower piedmont and coastal plains. Winter temperatures average in the low forties in the mountains and some ten degrees higher in the piedmont and coastal plains.[1]

HISTORICAL DATA, COLONIAL PERIOD

Here again, North Carolina is unique; first attempts of English to establish a settlement in North America were made in North Carolina. Although this early attempt was a failure, after Virginia, North Carolina was among the earliest states to be settled, by the English and other European countries.

The history of this state is quite long and varied, therefore, no attempt to go into details is made. Only some dates and important events are mentioned. Before the white man came, North Carolina was inhabited by native Americans, that we called "Indians". Catawba, Tuscaroras and the larger Cherokee Tribe, were the main groups of Indians here. It is likely that the Catawba Indians were the first natives that the English encountered when they tried to establish the first colonies.

A Florentine, Giovanni de Verrazano, explored sections of coastal North Carolina in 1524. Between 1540 and 1570, Spanish explorers, explored portions of western North Carolina.

---

1   Official Travel Guide of North Carolina (http://www.visitnc.com/travelpubs)

Two early attempts to establish permanent settlements in eastern North Carolina failed. The first permanent settlers came down from tidewater, Virginia.

North Carolina was named in honor of Charles the First, who granted a charter to eight English gentlemen in 1663. A second charter to clarify the first was granted in 1665. These gentlemen were known as Lords Proprietors that made the laws governing the territorial region. This system of government lasted until 1729, until the Crown, except the area that Lord Granville retained, purchased most of it. Therefore, two sets of government rules the state. This type of government ended when North Carolina became a state in 1776, under the Halifax Resolves, adopted by the 83 delegates to the Fifth Provincial Congress. This gave North Carolina its first constitution.[2]

EMERALDS

According to historians, emeralds were mined in Egypt over four thousand years ago. Queen Cleopatra treasured them, and later, so did the Roman Emperors.

The sixteenth century brought a profound change in the exposure and interest in owning these jewels. Spanish Conquistadors discovered the Indians of Columbia, South America to be mining and wearing emeralds. Some years after the discovery, the Spanish developed the Columbian mines and sold emeralds worldwide. They were treasured by royalty in India, Turkey and throughout Europe.

Columbia is one of the largest sources for quality emeralds. Other countries producing them are Brazil, Madagascar, Africa, India and Australia.

Emeralds are also mined in North Carolina. Some mines even permit the public to mine. Mines are located in Hiddenite, Little Switzerland and other locations.

Emeralds have been found in Jackson County, where this story is based upon.

---

2   The State Library of North Carolina   http://statelibrary.ncdcr.gov/nc/history/history.htm

http://www.ncwildlife.org/Plan/NC_River_Basins_Map.htm

PROLOGUE

Haunting the dark passes of the Great Smokey Mountains, Uktena, the great horned serpent use to lie in wait, in lonely places, to surprise its victims.

Cherokee legend

"Hey Bob, look down; we have a visitor; he wants to talk to you". I had just finished nailing a rafter in place and was poised to move along the scaffold to the next one, when Betty called from below. Glancing down, I saw a rather large man, standing at the foot of the ladder. "Oh! Hell," I thought; here I am, exposed like a possum out on a limb. Glancing towards Betty; she patted her apron, nodding assuredly, for underneath that apron was a 9mm Browning automatic, kept there for just such occasions as this. Buck, our big Airedale hung close by her side, ready to address any situation that might go sour.

Gingerly descending the ladder, I stopped on the first rung to face the man, eye-ball to eye-ball. Coppery skin, dark hair and eyes, high cheek-bones, "Got to be full-blood Cherokee" I thought.

"George Owl", he said, extending an oversized hand. "Bob Butler", I answered, as we shook hands. "Well, Mr. Butler, I heard that you had bought this property from my friends, the Norton's, and I came over to see if I could hunt on it." "What kind of game did you hunt?" I asked. "I hunt deer, bear, turkeys and small game like grouse quail, rabbits or squirrels." "There are lots of wild hogs up there on the mountain", he said. "Tell you what, George, let's go over to that lumber pile in the shade and we can talk; maybe my wife can bring us something to drink."

I'm getting ahead of this story, why don't we go back to the very beginning?

James M. Butler Family circa 1902

Leland	Levi	James M.	Virginia	M. C.		Estelle
			Eleanor	Texanna		
				Archie		

CHAPTER I

Pursuing a Dream

Following the close of World War II and upon receiving my discharge, I returned to the county of my birth. It was one of the smallest counties in North Carolina, where the mountains met the piedmont plateau, about equally. With a favorable climate and ample rainfall, apples, grapes and peaches were ideal crops.

My time in service had been spent overseas, flying against the Japanese in China and other Asiatic countries. Quite naturally, these countries, with their teeming millions, that we sometimes had to live in close proximity to, did not endear me to this life style. As a consequence, I was determined to live the balance of my life in a sparsely populated country. That is, if I were lucky enough to survive the war in a reasonably healthy state! I would seek out an area in the United States with lots of streams and mountains and large tracts of land.

Prior to the war, I had spent two and a half years in the Panama Canal Zone, working on defense housing for the military. This allowed me to save enough money for any future plans. Betty, my wife, had taught school during the war years, and together, we had saved a nice nest egg. She shared my vision, of a thinly populated country and beautiful scenery, where we could perhaps make a living and enjoy life, to the fullest.

In the late 1920's, our family would visit an aunt in Jackson County, North Carolina. Scenes of beautiful waterfalls, mountain and valleys flooded memories almost forgotten. Although very beautiful, my home country simply did not have large tracts of cheap land for sale. Could, the, Jackson County, be an ideal place to search out our dreams?

Jackson County, North Carolina, is in the southwestern part of the state, joining South Carolina and extending northward to the Cherokee Indian Reservation (Qualla Boundary). Fertile valleys, surrounded by high mountains and drained by the beautiful Tuckasegee River, it is one of the most attractive counties in North Carolina. Numerous waterfalls are an added attraction.

Highway #107comes out of South Carolina and runs northward through the county, Highway #64 runs eat-west and intersects #107 at the small town of Cashiers. Sylva, located in the northern part of Jackson, is the county seat. Elevations very greatly, from 1,850 feet to over 6,000 feet on the highest peaks. Winter temperatures average 40 °F while July temperatures average 76 °F. Rainfall will average 75", annually.

At the close of World War II, Jackson Country was sparsely populated, people had gone to the large cities to work in the defense industry and simply remained there. Who would want to return to a life of drudgery, working on farms or in the woods? There were few jobs for the remaining war veterans and they too sought work in factories that were switching over to civilian economy. With large tracts of cut over forests, Jackson seemed to be the ideal place to start our search.

Placing our house on the real estate market and packing clothes and other light necessities, we were now prepared to begin the search.

Early on a Monday morning in mid-September, we headed northwest towards Hendersonville. Throughout the war, Betty had driven a 1940 Ford coupe to school and it was in very good shape. I had bought a surplus army Jeep with low miles on it, so we were confident that these two vehicles would get us to our destination. Buck, our big Airedale, preferred to ride with me in the Jeep.

At Hendersonville, we turned west on #64 and proceeded towards Rosman. As we passed Rosman, the landscape began to change. Ahead of us in the distance, the Blue Ridge Mountains were showing their typical colors of hazy blue. As we climbed towards Lake Toxaway, the temperatures began to drop and the thought occurred to me that perhaps it was time to pull over and have lunch. We had been on the road some three hours without a break. Finding a wide shoulder in the road near the river that drains Lake Toxaway, we stopped and leisurely ate our lunch, while enjoying the scenery. Buck showed his appreciation for the lunch by gulping a salami sandwich in two bites.

Resuming the trip, we rolled into Cashiers at about one o'clock. We had planned well beforehand that Cashiers would be the center of temporary quarters. If we were lucky to find a place to rent; the stay in Cashiers might be long indeed, because there was no assurance that I could locate a large piece of forestland, just on the spur of the moment. Our first priority of the moment was to find lodging for the night.

Where is the first place to stop and inquire about anything when one is traveling in the countryside? Why of course, a service station. There it was, one the right side of the street. Mike's Gulf Service Station. A single old fashioned, glass cylinder pump, the kind that had to be hand-pumped, stood out like a beacon from a lighthouse, on the Outer Banks. Pulling up, I got out and walked into the office, since no one came out to service the Jeep.

No one in the office either, but I heard a metallic tinkering in the garage area. Sticking my head in there, I called "anyone here to give me gas?" "Just a second," a man answered, "be right with you." "Sorry about this, my help has gone to dinner and I'm swamped." The young man apologized as he crawled from the service pit.

Standing by the pump, as the Jeep was being serviced, I asked the man if there might be a place where we could spend the night. "Well, the only place that I can think of, is the Bumgarner place; they used to take in boarders." "It's on the other end of town-west." "Can't miss it, it's on the left side of the street and has three large gables." "My name is Mike Bryson, tell Mrs. Bumgarner that I sent you." "Thanks, Mike. I'm Bob Butler and this is my wife, Betty, we appreciate your help." We had used only 5 gallons total of gasoline in the two vehicles in almost four hours of driving. The bill was $1.25 just twenty-five cents a gallon – amazing!

As we drove through the village, I noticed only a few stores; what few that were in evidence were very small. One store stood out through a very large, two-storied building, evidently this must be a general store, I reasoned. "I want to see what's inside when I have some leisure time." I thought to myself.

The Bumgarner house was easy to spot and it was exactly as Mike Bryson had described. Three gables stood out, seemingly, to monitor the goings and comings of the town's people.

Ed Bumgarner's home place in Cashiers circa 1926

We parked, leaving Buck in the Jeep and walked up to the large porch; climbing the steps, I noticed several large rocking chairs. Evidently, the Bumgarners enjoy spending some time out there, I thought. The double front door, with frosted glass on it's upper half, had a twist-type doorbell. At several twists, I could hear footsteps approaching from inside. As the door swung open, a tall, dark-haired woman stood, staring, expectantly at us. "Mrs. Bumgarner?" I asked. "Yes, I'm Octa Bumgarner, could I help you?" "Well, Ma'am, I'm Robert Butler and this is my wife, Betty; Mike Bryson said that you might have a room to rent."

"Where are you folks from?" she asked. "We are from Polk County; that's a small county, towards the east." "Yes, I know where it is, my son-in-law lives there and he is also a Bulter." She answered. "Your son-in-law is my uncle." I nodded. "Oh my! Do come in and tell me about yourselves," Octa, laughed.

She waved us to a chair and wanted to know how long that we would be staying. "We would like to settle down in Jackson County, if we could buy a large tract of land and perhaps build on it," I began. "For the present, we're just looking for a room to rent until we have time to look around." "I have some rooms upstairs, I used to have a number of boarders, but";' my daughter is the only person that sleeps here, now."

Let's go up and I'll show you what we have." She led us to a large corner bedroom, a window in back and one on the west side, well illuminated the room. Betty examined the double bed and other furnishings and at length said that everything suited her fine. "We'll take it." She nodded.

"There is a single bath room upstairs, but my daughter is the only one that your would have to share it with." Octa commented. Well, Mrs. Bumgarner, how about meals included, that is, breakfast and supper?" Betty asked. "Oh that would include the room, breakfast and supper, I could include all, for ten dollars a week." "That sounds great, Mrs. Bumgarner, we'll be happy to board here for a while." Betty concluded. "We have a big dog with us, is there a shed outside that he could sleep in?" I asked. "Yes, 'round back, he can sleep there", she answered. Paying for a week in advance, we unloaded our belongings.

It was early afternoon and I was anxious to get in the Jeep and drive around; it would be some three and a half hours, before supper.

"Let's see what's in that big store, I suggested; later we might drive up #107." Betty agreed, and we drove to the store. It was two-storied, with lap-strake siding. A front porch without banisters, so that goods could be loaded or unloaded, was at the same elevation as a truck. The cool shade under the porch was also a haven for the town's dogs that might be hanging around! On either side of the double doors, a glass-front covered the first floor. All manner of goods were visible in the windows.

Inside, was a central counter, supporting several glass-lined cases and isles on each side ran the entire length of the building. Counters on both walls also extended almost the same distance. The first third of the floor was devoted to groceries, most of which were staples, such as can goods, flour, coffee, sugar, etc. Fresh meats were enclosed in a large, ice-cooled case. A smaller upright case contained milk and related products. The rear two-thirds of the store was the most interesting to me. It was full of clothes, shoes and tools that were suitable for gardening, general farming and hardware. I purchased a Case "cattleman" style pocketknife for six dollars. When I paid for the knife, the owner, a large, portly man, introduced himself as John Owen. As we chatted, I mentioned that we would be boarding with the

Bumgarners for a while. We had spent a good thirty minutes in the store, so it was time to see what was up on #107.

As we drove towards Glenville, looking towards the east, the high mountains were clearly visible, shrouded in the blue haze that clearly defined "The Blue Ridge Mountains"!

Glenville was just a wide place in the road. We stopped at the old iron bridge that spans a branch of the Tuckasegee River. Nothing had changed much, since I visited the Holdens, my mother's relatives, spending nights with Tommy Holden. The Holden House was visible from #107.

Continuing on up #107, we turned towards the east on #281 and parked where the road crossed the main branch of the Tuckasegee River. From this location, we could discern a vast expanse of forestlands, rising towards the mountains.

"Would it not be fantastic, if someday I could settle around here?" I dreamed. Betty jolted me from my daydream, by tapping my arm. "Remember, dinner is served at six." She reminded. Turning around, we drove back to Cashiers, stopping at the general store.

Buck needed to be fed and also he always drank a lot of water. I bought a dozen cans of Alaskan Salmon, his favorite food and also a wash pan for his water. At the time, salmon was only fifteen cents a can!

When we reached the Bumgarners, I fed Buck and told him to stay put; knowing full well that he would be in some mischief as soon as I turned my back!

Dinner that evening was served in the large dining room on a table that had been made to serve a large family. Octa, her husband, Elbert, and their youngest daughter, Soyrietta and we were unable to fill up the empty space of the large dining table.

It was quite evident that Mrs. Bumgarner had made a special effort on our behalf! The food was not only varied, but so delicious! There was baked chicken, mashed potatoes, green beans squash, tomatoes, corn on the cob, etc. Desert was black berry cobbler, for they grew their own berries. I enjoyed the meal so much that I couldn't help but feel a pang of guilt for paying so little for the room and board!

Conversation around the table was mostly directed about us, mostly, I imagined because of our connection with my uncle. Soyrietta taught school and when she learned that Betty was a teacher, the two really struck a friendship.

The Bumgarners had raised a large family of four girls and two boys. All were living elsewhere, except Soyietta. Elbert was in the lumber business and he became very interested when I mentioned some of my logging experiences, down in South Carolina on the great Santee River lowlands.

They were very interested to learn that we would like to settle somewhere in Jackson County, if land were available. "Yes," Elbert said, "there is plenty of cutover forest land that you can buy." "Lumbermen around here are interested in buying timber and not the land." "They have to operate on a day-to-day basis, so they certainly don't want to tie themselves up with a lot of land." "Maybe I can help you," he concluded.

We talked about the chances of buying a house in Cashiers, but Elbert said that he didn't know of a single house for sale. Octa spoke up at once, "Say Elbert, you know we have that boarded-up store on the other side of town and we have no further use for it." "It's a tax burden for us; if it were fixed up, it would make a nice temporary home for someone." "Well, why don't you show it to Bob and Betty." He replied.

After breakfast the next morning, Betty drove Mrs. Bumgarner over to the store, Buck and I followed in the Jeep.

The store sat on a large lot, in fact two acres. Mike's Service Station was plainly in view, some two hundred yards distance. The building was similar in construction to the large general store that we had visited yesterday; although only half its' size. Two storied, with a painted tin roof, it was still large enough to serve as a general store for a small community, as Cashiers. A front porch, without banisters, once served as a platform, where goods were loaded or unloaded. The ground floor was glass fronted, where goods or hardware were once viewed from the outside. Double doors were now nailed shut, so we had to enter the building from the rear.

As Octa unlocked the back, we entered a room that once served as a kitchen. A sink and a large cook stove were the sole furnishings. The adjoining room was once the bedroom; no furnishings, except a small dresser was around. Octa said that we could spend as much time as we cared, but she had to get back to her housework; so Betty drove her back.

Meanwhile, I entered the large commercial room in front. Two large wooded counters ran close to both walls, leaving enough space for a person to move along taking care of customers.

A wide stairway, against the part of the west wall led to the second floor. Buck and I climbed the stairs into semi-darkness, for the single windows on either end emitted little light and I had to wait several minutes to adjust to the surroundings. Two single light bulbs hung from the ceiling. The insulation was so frayed that the naked wire was visible in places. "Boy!" I thought, "If the switch were turned on now, this place would go up like a bomb!"

Two large, dusty tables were the only furnishings that were visible, but trash was everywhere and there was no telling what else I could see with the poor light. Obviously, the building would first have to be rewired before very much could be done to restore it to livable condition.

Descending the stairs, I walked out back. An outdoor privy stood at the far end of the lot. A small utility building, part of which was only a shed to store firewood, stood close to the house. A well, with an iron hand pump, reminded me of a slim teapot, with its' spout, drooping downward. An electric pump would have to replace this iron man killer!

Presently, Betty returned. "I stopped at the big store and bought lunch; salami, bread, mayonnaise and tomatoes." She beamed. "Wasn't I smart?" "Yeah, but what about drinks?" I joked. "Oh, I didn't think about that." She apologized, "I'll run down to Mike's and get some cokes." "Well, just wait a while, it's not quite time to eat, you can get them later and they will be cold." I answered.

The early September weather was just like August and the heat was getting to us. "Let's go find some shade and not have to smell this musty building." I suggested. We found a spot under a large white pine that was barren of weeds and chiggers, and sat for a while, discussing things that would have to be done to put this building into a livable condition. "The big items would be a bathroom and a septic tank with drain field, rewiring the building, electrifying the well and installing a hot water heater." I said. "Yes, but we need a bed and a small refrigerator, too." Betty added.

Our stomachs had reminded us that time had flown by and it was time to eat. Betty and Buck left for Mike's and were back shortly with ice-cold cokes. She sliced tomatoes and made sandwiches. Buck's thick salami was minus the tomato. "Sorry about that old boy." I patted him, "but you ain't nothing but An old hound dawg!" We ate leisurely and later rested for a long spell under the large white pine. I must have fallen asleep, for Betty woke me and said that it was time to go back to the Bumgarner's.

At dinner that evening, Elbert asked if we had looked at the building. "Yes, Octa showed it and we spent most of the day there, going over things that would need to be done to it, to make it livable." I answered. "Well, I realize it will take some money to do that, so if you want it, we'll let you have it for $500." I turned to Betty, "What do you think?" I asked. "It's like this Bob, I like Cashiers and it's the only place for sale. Let's take a chance! We'll take it, Elbert." I concluded Octa clapped her hands, "I'm so glad you two are going to be with us." She beamed. "Friday, I had to go over to Ashville and pick up some parts for the mill; I'll stop by my lawyers in Sylva and he can prepare the deed."

A week after Elbert had informed his lawyer to prepare a deed for the store, we drove to Sylva to consummate the transaction. Meanwhile, as soon as Elbert and I agreed to the sale to us, Betty and I drove to Sylva and found an electrician, who was now busy rewiring the store. We also found a contractor to put in the septic tank system. Cold weather was only two months away, time was precious and we had to work every waking hour. We couldn't find an electric well pump and other items in Sylva, so this required a trip to Ashville. Betty wanted a small electric store and refrigerator; I figured that we had better keep the big wood range, just in case. With all this equipment, in addition to a hot water heater, the kitchen was somewhat crowded.

The last big thing was a bathroom, which I could build, myself. Elbert had a supply of dry hemlock framing lumber and I started a twenty-by-twenty foot building. The outside was white pine with Douglas fir plywood panels for the inside. Hemlock sub-floor was covered with three-quarter inch fir plywood. The floor was finished off with composition tile. A contractor put in the plumbing and fixtures. Well, I surmised, this wasn't the fanciest building, but it went up fast with the plywood and pre-cut framing!

By November twenty, we were able to move into our new "home". It had been quite a struggle, dealing with contractors, running to and fro, and trying to work, myself. Now, we were ready for a short vacation!

I had worked in Wilmington, North Carolina at one time; buying hardwood logs for a plywood company. One source of logs was the Barnes lumber company. They used cypress and pine timber in their operation and were glad to sell their red and tupelo gum logs to us. The owner, Fred Barnes, and I became friends, and Rachel, his wife, and Betty were also close. They urged us to visit them on many occasions after we moved from Wilmington. So placing a call from the only pay phone in Cashiers, I called Fred. "Sure, we'll look forward to having you." Fred had invited.

We certainly needed a short vacation, short enough to return and prepare for the start of winter, only a month away.

Packing enough belongings for a three night's stay, we left early the next morning; it was Friday, the last week of October. Taking #107 south, the scenery began to change as we descended the Jackson County highlands. White pines and hemlocks, which forested the uplands, gave way to piedmont species, such as short leaf pines and a variety of more hardwoods. Breathtaking colors in the piedmont were due to the many species, such as red maple, sweet and black gums, many different oaks and under-storied sourwoods and dogwoods.

Turning east on #123 in South Carolina, we passed Greenville and headed on towards Spartanburg. All this area, from Greenville and Spartanburg is known as peach country. For here, on the weathered granite red clay, grow the finest peaches in the country. No other peaches grown elsewhere in the United States have the particular fine flavor as these peaches.

From Spartanburg, we took #29 to Charlotte and stopped there for lunch. I asked the cashier at the restaurant if a large hamburger could be prepared for Buck and they gladly obliged.

From Charlotte, #74 runs to Wilmington and as we gradually left the lower piedmont, mixed hardwood forests, large farms and extensive areas of pine forests began to appear. An industry of naval stores, based on vast forests of longleaf pine, once was prevalent in the coastal plains. Ever wonder where North Carolinians got the name "Tar Heels?"

What seemed like a century, eventually, Wilmington loomed ahead. The city is one of two important seaports in North Carolina.

Reached by rail, highways and ships, it is and important industrial hub for the state.

The Barnes lived two blocks south of Market Street, in a quiet neighborhood, their large brick house, similar to others there, reflected the success of Fred's business. From the appearance of this house, the lumber business had certainly been good to Fred!

Large pines and magnolias surrounded a two storied, columned house; the spacious front porch, lending an atmosphere of "southern solitude". A large double car garage served also as a workshop for Fred's hobbies. As Betty viewed the gleaming Mercedes parked in the garage, she whispered, "Quite a contrast to our little Ford, eh?" "Shouldn't you have married for money, instead of love?" I kidded.

As we rang the doorbell, a light skinned Negro maid, dressed in a starchly uniform, opened the door. Rachel had just entered from the back with an armload of flowers from her garden and she greeted us with gusto. "Let me put these down. I'll be right with you."

As soon as we had been seated, the maid came in with a large tray of ice tea and cookies. Suddenly, I remembered poor Buck and asked Rachel if Buck could stay on the front porch. "Of course." And instructed the maid to bring a bowl of water for him. Buck had been wedged against the car door and immediately went through a series of stretches on the porch.

As we sat for a time, reminiscing over old times, presently Fred came in; Friday, like Monday, was a hard day at the mill and he was fatigued. "There must be an easier way to make a living, than running a sawmill." He sighed. "From the looks of Rachel's diamonds and other jewelry, I suspected that poor Fred would eventually work himself into the grave, I thought. "Well, it's great to see you; it's been some time since." He continued.

Rachel, with help of her maid, had prepared dinner and after we had showered and dressed, dinner was served. Later we sat up and more relaxed now, talked and sipped a few drinks, until late.

After breakfast the next morning, Fred drove me over to the mill; Rachel and Betty would shop for a while and then go to their house on the beach. We would spend Saturday and Sunday there.

The sawmill was ideally located to receive logs by truck, rail and water. It stood adjacent to Smith Creek. Barges loaded with cypress, pine and hardwood, would come in from vast reaches of the Cape Fear,

11

Black River and North East Cape Fear Rivers. The hardwood logs were not sawn, but were sold to other mills.

The mill itself was the state of the art, as mills go. With a four foot band saw and several re-saws, production averaged thirty-five thousand board feet of lumber a day.

The office, with walls paneled in old growth cypress, displayed paintings of various hunting scenes, indicating to a visitor that Fred's chief hobby was duck hunting. A mahogany desk and two leather chairs and a large steel safe, took up most of the room.

We sat for a long time in the office, after touring the mill. Mostly, we talked about the timber business. Fred could not understand why we would want to move to the far mountains in Jackson County and give up a place like Wilmington. "How in Hell are you going to make a living up there?" He shook his head. "I'll put Betty to teaching and loaf around." I joked. "Seriously, if I can find enough of cheap, cut-over land, I'll make a living." I answered. "Well, right now the lumber business is fine, but the competition for saw timber is pressing; there are two other sawmills in Wilmington and two paper companies. Besides, other companies are in here looking for timber." "Fortunately, I have a good mill manager because I have to spend as much time looking for timber, as I do in the mill." "Well, let's go to Wrightsville Beach and join the girls."

Wrightsville Beach only stretches a little over a mile, but without doubt, it is the nicest beach in North Carolina. Many of the houses, although of earlier style, nether the less, are well made and in excellent condition. They are principally owed by people who live in, or around, Wilmington. With nice restaurants that are famous for serving fresh seafood that comes from Maine to Florida, the most discriminating diner can expect the best. This is not only during the summer, but year round!

The Barnes house was located midway along the beach; with a screened porch, they could view the beach, catch the breezes from the water and be protected from flying insects.

Saturday afternoon was a beautiful, clear fall day; the water still warm enough for bathers and there were plenty of them, enjoying the surf. After a light lunch, we donned our swimsuits and joined the crowd. Most of the afternoon we spent just going in or out of the water and lying under a large beach umbrella. Neither, Betty or I had a tan and when not in the water, we stayed in the shade. Buck was busy much of the time chasing crabs.

We showered and dressed early; Fred had called the restaurant for reservations. During weekends, one was lucky to be seated, if they had no reservations. Faircloths, located right on the Inland Waterway, was also a large marina and perhaps the most famous.

Entering the restaurant, we were immediately placed at a table where the boat traffic could be observed. The menu was so large and varied, so enticing, that it was hard to decide on what to order, especially Betty and me, who lived far from this gourmet diner's heaven! Fred and Rachel, so used to seafood, ordered steaks. Betty decided on fried flounder and crab cakes, I chose a huge seafood platter, including fried flounder, fried shrimp and oysters.

We ate leisurely, all the while conversing about our plans, or what the future for people engaged in the forest industry, around Wilmington. Fred talked about his trips to New York, where he had several lumber accounts. Often Rachel would accompany him and spend much time shopping. I imagined that Rachel must spend much time buying jewelry and clothing. It had been a delightful evening, one that Betty and I would long remember.

Sunday, Fred had to dress for church, the First Baptist in Wilmington; for today he had to usher. This was one reason that I trusted and admired his integrity. Sunday afternoon was the repeat of Saturday, most of our time we spent on the beach. Crowds were larger today, probably to enjoy the water while there was such short time left.

I had to give Buck a good washing under the hose to get the salt from his kinky hair. We spent the evening on the porch and turned in for the day, after bidding Fred good-bye, as he had to get up early and go to the mill.

Monday, we left for Cashiers around nine o'clock. Throughout the long trip home, I kept wondering if I had done the right thing for Betty, dragging her off to an area as rugged as Jackson County, where only the hardy people could survive! Too, should I had gone into business with Fred? Perhaps we would be enjoying the good life, with nice surroundings. Oh, well! Things were already set; we had made a decision, now it was too late. We rolled into Cashiers around six o'clock.

We had intended to sleep late, but early Tuesday morning, Buck woke us, whining and scratching to get out. As I opened the back door, a heavy frost greeted me. Glancing towards the wood shed, I could see only a week or two of stove wood left. I realized that I had to get a winter's supply of wood, and soon!

Fortunately, there were a few armloads of wood next to the big kitchen range and I quickly built a fire. After it was burning well enough, I went back to bed and waited until the kitchen and bedroom were comfortably heated. As long as we kept the door shut between the kitchen and the store section, the kitchen stove would easily heat the kitchen and bedroom.

As the rooms warmed, we got up and Betty started breakfast, while I brewed coffee. In the span of a few minutes, I sat by the stove, staring out the window and sipped the coffee; my mind wandering back to the same scene of childhood days. Betty announced that breakfast was ready and this jolted me back to the present.

I had remembered that Elbert sawed a lot of white oak lumber that he sold to a flooring plant near Rosman. The mountains of hardwood slabs were sawn into twelve-inch blocks and sold as fuel. However, the buyer had to split the blocks for a cook stove, whole blocks though, could be burned in a heater. Betty agreed to meet me at the general store, when I was through with Elbert.

Buck and I got in the Jeep and drove to the sawmill; it was located adjacent to #64, a half mile west of Cashiers. The log yard was full of white pine and hemlock logs; he's getting ready for winter, I reasoned. Deep snows could virtually shut down a logging operation. Elbert was in his small office and he greeted me warmly as I walked in. "Well, are you about settled in?" He asked. "Yes, we're about squared away, but need to buy enough slab blocks for the winter." "I have plenty, how soon do you need the wood?" "Oh, whenever you can deliver them." I answered. "I sell them by the dump truck load, that's about a half cord, that is easily enough for a month's supply. "Right now my man is delivering a load, but I'll put him on yours when he gets back." I get ten dollars a load." "Well, have him deliver me six loads, that should see us through the winter." I paid for the wood and asked him to tell the driver to dump the wood next to the wood shed, in back of the house.

We sat and talked for a few minutes and Elbert asked if I was still in mind to buy a large tract of land. "Yes, I sure am." I replied. "That's what we came up here for." "Well, when you get time, go over and see John Norton, he and his wife are in poor health and they can't take care of their place. They should really get a small place in Sylva, where they could get to a doctor." Elbert described where they lived. He also said that I should talk to Frank Holden. "He's got lots of land and his sons run heavy equipment and are building logging roads for lots of loggers. "I'm sure that he knows some land owners of large cut-over tracts." "Anyway Bob, we'll try to help you locate some land." I thanked Elbert for his advise and went on to the general store.

When I entered the store, Betty was busy, filling her grocery list, so I walked to the rear and looked at some axes. There were several brands, so I found a Kelly with a straight handle. I also picked a nice Collins axe, with a good handle. Gloves were a must for my hands, otherwise, I could expect blisters. I found a pair of soft leather gloves that fitted my hands. The axes and gloves were just twelve dollars.

When we got home, the first load of firewood was just being unloaded. I asked the driver if he would throw on a short log or an extra thick slab about six feet long that would serve as a chopping block. After lunch, when the second load came with the chopping black, I began splitting the wood for the cook stove; blocks for the big heater in the storeroom could be burned, as they were. After two hours of splitting, my fingers were so cramped that I could hardly hold the axe, so I gave up for the day. I would work for a couple of hours, then rest for an hour and continue on for another two hours. It would take several weeks to split enough wood for the kitchen stove to last the winter.

It was now approaching mid-November and there was a decided change in the air. Frosts became more severe, leaves, once splashed with their spell binding colors were now cloaked in the dab brown of late fall. Smoke from the chimneys, seemed to solidify into lazy spirals as it drifted skyward. Yes, winter was just over a few ridges!

Monday morning, I made up a small knapsack of food, several c cans of Vienna sausage, saltine crackers, a half loaf of bread, a small jar of peanut butter and a pound of coffee. An army canteen and cup, a small belt axe, the Case pocketknife, matches and a Ruger 22 pistol, with a box of cartridges made up the list. I carried a compass and a pedometer in my shirt pocket. With the pedometer, I could roughly measure the distance and the compass would keep me on a straight line. I wanted Buck to stay with Betty, but she would have none of it. She said that if I were to have an accident, Buck could go warn someone, so there! Buck went with me.

Following #107 to where it intersected #281, we turned east and followed #281 until the Norton mailbox was spotted. So far, so good, with Elbert's directions. Turning up a well-graveled road between two fenced pastures, the road was in good shape, until we entered the forests. Here the road became rutted and uneven, tire tracks were not recent, but perhaps two or three weeks old. We continued on for at least two miles and came to a wooden bridge, which spanned a beautiful, crystal clear creek. I was forced to stop on the bridge and see if there were any trout in the clear water; I saw none, but still admired the scene. Continuing on, I spied a large red barn, then the Norton house a few dozen yards ahead.

The Norton Place

Ordering Buck to remain in the Jeep, I got out and went to the front door. The blaring sound of a radio, drowned out my knocking on the door. "Hell." I thought. "These people couldn't hear a bomb go off!" After a few moments of knocking, I went to the front window and tapped on it; this did the trick for presently a man opened the door.

A stooped, elderly man asked what I wanted. "Mr. Norton?" I asked. "I'm Robert Butler and I came over to talk to you about some land." Your name Butler, eh?" "Yes sir, I'm Robert Butler." "Well, come in." He invited.

An elderly woman sat by the fireplace, in a large recliner; a blanket covered most of her legs and upper body. She kept her eyes on me, but didn't offer to speak. I figured that she wasn't well, neither physically, nor mentally. Norton wanted to know where I was from and then asked why I was looking for some land to buy. "Well, I've got plenty of land, that's for sure." "Yes, I would sell at the right price and a house over in Sylva to boot." Well, that's interesting, Mr. Norton, give me a few days to look at your land, then maybe we can talk." He then described the boundaries of his property. It was bounded on three sides by creeks most of the way, then by a wire fence on the other side of the mountain. I then told him that I might have to spend the night on the mountain and he cautioned, that there were varmints up there – bears, snakes, wild boars. I told him not to worry, I had my big dog with me and I would be safe. "Now, you be careful." He advised.

We left the Jeep in the yard and walked a half-mile to the bridge, then, staying off the creek a ways for a better footing, we followed upward. Keeping to as straight a line as possible, so the pedometer would give me a correct reading, the land began to steepen the farther up we went. For what seemed like three hours, we came to the beginning of the great mountain pass. Here, by a large pool, we rested for a long time; I bathed my face in the icy liquid and drank my fill of the water; Buck filled his stomach, with the sound of a bear trap, closing.

The Pass

Norton had described the old Indian trail, which led upward through the pass. For centuries, it had been used by Native Americans as they went from one valley to the next. White pines, hemlocks and red spruce, at first grew tall, but as we progressed upward, they began to get smaller and smaller. A thick growth of rhododendron lined the creek and it, too, became smaller. After another hour, we reached the top and were surprised to find the very top, somewhat level. Here, again, a long rest was welcomed.

Now we started downward, along the ancient trail; it was very steep and we had to be very careful; it always seems that going down is much harder than climbing. Following the trail downward for a mile, we came to a shallow shelve that extended both east and west, and just below the shelve, we came to a corner fence.

Now, turning westward, we followed the old fence for maybe a half-mile, until we came to a small waterfall. As it was getting up into the mid afternoon, I decided that we would rest and the start back. To be caught this high on the mountain at night, would not be pleasant.

A small sandy pool at the bottom of the waterfall looked like a good place to fill my canteen and get a drink. Stooping over, I began to fill the canteen and suddenly, I spied something bright red in the bottom of the pool. Reaching down, I picked up a beautiful, transparent garnet.

Not only was it so transparent, it was the color of a red cranberry. Excited, I began searching in the sand and found several more. They seemed to be all over the place and I had a pocket full before I noticed the time. We've got to leave, I said to Buck.

Out along the fence line we hurried, taking care not to fall. Twenty minutes later, we turned upward at the fence corner. A hard climb to the top of the pass took another forty-five minutes; there we were forced to catch out breaths. I couldn't see the sun now because it was behind the mountain peak to my left, so it was hard to tell how long it would be until sunset.

We got to our feet and rushed down the pass and thirty minutes later we arrived at the pool, where the old Indian trail turned westward. Following this for some twenty minutes, we suddenly came to a huge overhang. Large enough to hold a medium sized house, the floor was covered with ashes and chunks of wood. This must be the place that Norton had mentioned. The sun had just set and darkness was only a few minutes away.

Rushing around, I gathered all the wood that I could find, for we had to spend the night here and fire would keep us from freezing. Shortly, I had a blazing fire going, hoping all the while, that the wood would last all night. Relaxing against the overhang wall, I opened the pack and found some cans of Vienna sausage and slices of bread. Splitting all this with Buck, it was wolfed-down in short order. I made a half canteen cup of coffee and sipped this; it seemed to sweep away the tiredness.

The night was a long one, every two hours, I had to feed the fire. The big dog nestled close to me and that kept some of the cold in check. It seemed that daylight would never come and the wood was nearly gone when it finally began to get lighter. I was sore and stiff, and could hardly stand at first; it took some time before I could take a few steps.

I found the last of the sausages and bread, and made a half canteen cup of coffee; it would be a longtime before the next meal.

Shouldering the small pack, we followed the old trail, westward, along the base of the towering peak, above us. A forty-five minute walk brought us to the westward boundary creek. From here, we turned downward, for nearly two hours, until we came to the large bottom creek. The going was rough along the larger creek, for the fine farmland had now grown up in a jungle of saplings and vine. Several deer got up, well ahead, we only caught a glimpse of their flags, as they crashed through the thick growth.

Now, we could hear the eastern boundary creek ahead and at the intersection with the large stream, we followed the smaller creek to the wooden bridge. The Norton house came into view, some twenty minutes later, as we followed the road.

As we approached the house, Norton was outside, trying to split wood for his large kitchen range. Poor fellow! He had difficulty in striking the same spot with the axe. Tired as I was, I offered to split some wood for him; but, laying the axe aside, he asked how we fared last night. "Well, it was a little chilly, but we kept a fire going and things weren't too bad." We talked for a spell, I asked about his wife and he replied that she seemed a little better. "I have a pretty good idea of how the boundary lines run; tomorrow, I'll be back and look at the interior of the land." Buck and I left for Cashiers.

Betty was in the kitchen, preparing a meal for us, when we walked in. I noted some apprehension in her voice, as she greeted us. "I expect you were cold last night. Did you find shelter to sleep under?" "We camped under a big overhang cliff, where the Indians used to spend the night and a little fire kept us from freezing." "Next time you spend the night on the mountain, you take your sleeping bag." She demanded. Reaching in the knapsack, I pulled out a handful of garnet and held them up for her to see. "Why they're beautiful." She gasped. "They would make a nice piece of jewelry."

"When we go over to Ashville again, let's try to find you a kit, so you can make some bracelets or something, because there are plenty of these stones on the mountain." Attacking the food ravishingly, we made short work of it, for it had been early morning since the slight two cans of Vienna sausages were a poor substitute for breakfast. Taking a shower later, I laid down for a while. I planned to run three cruise line across the width of the property, these would be one half mile apart and the timber wouldn't be tallied. A rough picture of what was one the most productive part of the property was all I needed.

Next morning, I stopped close to the bridge and paced some three hundred yards up the mountain; here I turned on a ninety degree bearing from the creek and began the first cruise line. Walking as fast as safety would allow, the bottom of the apple orchard came into view some twenty minutes later. Forty-five minutes later, I had reached the western boundary creek. Stands of young white pine had been encountered in the shallow hollows and on the drier ridges, white oak, hickory, and lesser species of hardwoods, prevailed. Turinng upward at the end of the first line, I paced some eight hundred steps, which would put me roughly a half mile above the first cruise line. A compass bearing of ninety degrees off the creek, would guide me across the property to the east boundary creek. Timber along the way seemed to be about the same as that on the first cruise line. When the east boundary creek was reached, I reversed the procedure on the top line and was finished by noon.

Walking diagonally down the mountain, I came out within a few yards of the Norton house. I reasoned that there would be at least four to five million board feet of white pine within ten years. Various species of oak, poplar, basswood, buckeye, birch and miscellaneous trees, would, at the present, amount to two thousand board feet per acre. Norton was in the yard when I came up and he waved me over to the porch. "Well, Mr. Butler, are you about finished with your walking?" "Yes sir, I'm pretty well finished." "Well, what do you think? Are you still interested in the property?" "Mr. Norton, that depends on the price for the land and you said that you wanted a house, also." I answered. "Well, if you want the property, I'll take ten dollars an acre for what the deed calls for and I would have to be satisfied with the house in Sylva." "How soon." I asked. "Would you want to settle up and move to Sylva?" "Just as soon as we can find a house in Sylva." He nodded. "In that case sir, I suggest that my wife come with me tomorrow, to stay with Mrs. Norton, then, you and I can go on to Sylva and start looking for a house that suits you." "That sounds fair enough." He answered.

The following morning, Betty and I were at the Norton's by eight o'clock. Betty had brought her own lunch and food for Buck. A chilly November day suggested that if we were to close the deal, and get the Norton's moved before winter settled in, there was no time to spare! We left promptly and were in Sylva by a quarter after nine.

Driving down Main Street, we spotted three real estate companies; I chose the one that was displayed as "CHEROKEE AUCTION & REALTY CO." A large, dark blue Lincoln, parked in front, suggested that the concern must be quite successful! As we entered the office, a middle-aged secretary waved us to a chair and advised that the realtor would be right out.

Presently, a strikingly beautiful, dark-haired young woman appeared and invited us into her office. She must be part Cherokee at least, I thought. Seated, as my eyes swept the room; many pictures of Jackson County's landscapes suggested that she handled real estate all over the county. After I explained what we were looking for, the lady pulled a folder from her desk and examined several pages. "You're in luck, I have several nice bungalows listed and are conveniently located. Let's go take a look."

Norton insisted that I ride up front, so that I could hear what the lady was saying; I couldn't argue the point, but did have difficulty keeping my eyes from wondering toward her nice tanned legs! She explained that there were few jobs in Sylva and people had moved elsewhere, so there were quite a few houses for sale.

Stopping at the first house was a waste of time; it had a garage, but no front porch, Norton insisted on that. We made several stops, but each house failed to please Norton, and I was becoming discouraged that nothing would please him. Finally, near the edge of town, we stopped at a house with a front porch and an open garage. Producing a key, the lady opened the front door and led us inside. It was a three-bedroom house with a kitchen-dining room combination. A small, screened in back porch seemed to attract Norton. Included with the package were an electric stove and refrigerator. An oil furnace also was pleasing, so we walked out back and examined the garage. "I could have doors put on the garage." Norton said. At that point, I knew that he was pleased with the house. "I believe this is what I want, how soon can we settle?" He wanted to know. "Well, Mr. Norton, let's go to the office and see how much this is going to cost me." I answered.

Back in the office, the realtor studied her folder and finally said the house was really worth six thousand dollars, but the owner agreed to let it go for four thousand, since it had been on the market for some time. "If this is what Mr. Norton wants, then I will buy it for him." Very well then, I'll put the lawyer on the legal work this afternoon." "Will you see that the water and electricity are turned on?" I requested the lady. She agreed that everything would be taken care of. "Now Mr. Norton, let's go see your lawyer and have him prepare a deed to your property." "Oh, by the way, do you know of a mover?" I asked the realtor. She consulted a directory and made a phone call. "He can get to you day after tomorrow." She said. Still holding the phone, she gave directions to the Norton place. Thanking the realtor for her time, we left for the Norton's lawyer.

After Norton's lawyer assured us the deed would be ready for signing by Friday, four days hence, we left and drove to the "Coffee Shop"; a restaurant that served home cooked meals. Both of us were hungry and we ordered country style steak, with mashed potatoes, green peas, corn bread and ice tea. This was topped off with apple pie for desert. I told Norton that we needed some packing boxes for his dishes, tableware and kitchen utensils. Stopping at a large grocery store, I asked the manager for some empty cardboard boxes and he led us to the back and told us to help ourselves.

After packing all the boxes inside each other that were possible, I crammed the lot in the car's trunk and we left for home. Once arriving at the Norton house, we spent the afternoon packing household goods in the boxes. Tomorrow it would take the entire day to finish the packing.

Back in Cashiers that night, Betty and I talked over the situation and she was concerned that the price for the land was "awfully" high and on top of that, we also had to pay for the Norton house. "Well, look at it this way, twenty thousand for the Norton property might sound high, but this is based on the deed description, not an actual survey." "As best as I could, I carefully paced the distance and the pedometer indicated that the average length was five miles, and the width, one and a half miles." "Now, that is seven and one half square miles, or around 4,800 acres." "Now dear lady, put that in your pipe and smoke it." "We're paying on the basis of the deed description of two thousand acres." "Oh, I didn't know that." Betty said, obviously relieved.

The next day, we were at the job by eight o'clock. There were just enough boxes to hold the small household goods, dishes, flat ware, kitchen culinary and numerous other small items. Clothes had to be packed and bundled up in sheets. By the end of the day, we were dead tired.

The movers showed up the next morning by nine o'clock with two large trucks, a regular movers van could not be brought in on account of the road. In two hours flat, they were ready and we all left for

Sylva. We began unpacking as soon as the movers had set up the beds, furniture and other large items. At noon, I drove down to the Coffee Shop and got some take out food for the four of us. Buck ate his hamburger on the porch. After lunch, we continued the unpacking and were mostly finished by five o'clock. Buck went with Betty and I followed in the Jeep. We stopped at the Coffee Shop and ordered a large meal for us and another hamburger for Buck, which he ate in the Jeep. Afterwards, we were never so tired and relieved to finally get to Cashiers, and home.

On Monday morning, Betty and I drove to Sylva. We had to take both vehicles, since the Norton's would ride with Betty to the lawyers' office and I followed in the Jeep. After signing and paying both parties, we returned to Cashiers.

That night at home, Betty and I sat up until late; we were so tired and excited that finally we had found our land. The land that we would put roots down in. For better or worse, there was no turning back!

CHAPTER II

Settling In

"Well Bob, are you ready to go?" Betty asked. "Go? Why we just went." "No, silly, not that." She laughed, "I mean, let's get some stuff together and spend a few nights at the Norton place, I want to see what we've bought; we could go up on the mountain and camp at the Overhang that you talked about." "Are you really up to that? It will be a hard climb and very cold." "Bob, the weather report says it will be warm for the next few days and I want to see where you got those beautiful stone; beside, when we get back to the house, you can hunt some fresh meat." "Well, if you are up to it, then let's go, it's your decision."

After breakfast, we made a list of supplies, for to be caught on the mountain without adequate food or supplies, if a snow should occur, would not be a pleasant experience. We would have to use the Jeep, at least it would get us there and back, but the ride would be chilly, indeed. Packing sleeping bags, two wool blankets and warm jackets, would keep our bodies warm at night. A full size axe, belt axe, hunting and pocket knives, folding shovel, canteen and flashlight, completed the hard list, except I would take my .22 Ruger pistol. I would take along my 12-gauge shotgun, but leave it at the Norton house.

Betty made up the food list. Flour, meal, sugar, coffee, rice, onions and potatoes were the basics. For breakfast, bacon, eggs, salt pork, grits and two loaves of bread; she also included a pancake mix and maple syrup. For the trip up the mountain, small cans of sausages, crackers, coffee, bread and sandwich meats, would have to suffice. Buck's fare

25

would be the usual – canned salmon. Betty's small battery powered radio, was a must to give us weather reports.

We left in the late afternoon, just in time before dark, so as to allow enough time to get settled in the Norton house. The first night would be spent there, then, we would leave early the next morning for the mountain.

I brought in several armloads of stove wood for the big kitchen range, while Betty was trying to tidy up one of the bedrooms. Presently, she hollered out "I didn't bring a broom; the dust is an inch thick in here." "Don't worry, I'll get you a broom in short order." I promised.

Going to the orchard, I cut dry broom sedge and compressed it into a comfortable handgrip, then Betty found some old grocery string, which I bound the thick part of the stems into a handle. I had seen the mountain people make their brooms this way. Betty seemed pleased with the item, at least she didn't complain.

The Norton's had taken all the chairs and had left only an old table on the back porch. I had remembered that the old barn had been used as a packinghouse for apples, so I walked down to it and with some efforts, opened the huge door enough to squeeze inside.

Windows on the sides emitted enough light to see by and there were apple boxes scattered everywhere. Selecting the two most sturdy, I pushed them out the narrow opening and carried them to the house; now, we had something to sit on! I started a fire in the kitchen range; the bedroom was off to the left, so heat from the stove would give us some warmth for at least an hour after we retired.

Betty fixed a light meal for supper, and afterward, we sat around the stove, planning out trip for tomorrow. Stoking the big stove with as much wood that it would hold, we spread our sleeping bags on the hard floor, at least, the Camp Overhang would be softer with a dirt floor than this place, I assured Betty.

Needless to say, we slept fitfully, tossing and turning, trying to get comfortable. Daylight was a welcome relief! The stove was barely warm, with just a few hot coals left, but I quickly brought them back to life and soon had a nice fire going. Then I crawled back into my sleeping bag until the kitchen heated. After a bit, I got up and put the coffee on and a few minutes later, was drinking its life-rejuvenating flavor. Betty joined me, "My shoulder is killing me." She complained. "Well, you made the decision to come." I reminded her. "Just shut up and pour me some coffee." She demanded. This seemed to smooth her feathers, as we sipped after sipped the steaming liquid. Feeling better now, my wife went after her duties, as only a woman can, she made scrambled eggs, bacon and pancakes. The huge breakfast would sustain us until we reached the Overhang. We finished out meal in silence, fearing that a few words might set off a tirade of complaints about the night.

As soon as the sun had reached the lower levels, we started our climb towards the Overhang. Our gear was heavy, but necessary, although it did slow us considerably. Forced to rest constantly, it was late morning by the time the Overhang was reached. At least we could travel up the pass and towards the other side, with much of our gear stashed at the Overhang.

I took the axe and began chopping some dead, dwarf oaks that previous ice storms had killed. We would not have time after our return to stagger in the darkness trying to find wood and certainly lots would be needed to keep us from freezing tonight.

I had enough wood, hopefully, in an hours time and at eleven, we set off along the old Indian trail, towards the pass. The trail turned abruptly upward as we entered the pass. Betty was amazed with the size of the hemlock and red spruce trees, with their immense under story of rhododendron. A few dozen yards up the pass, the path suddenly narrowed between several immense boulders. "What a likely place for a snake or something to hide and way lay a victim." I said. "Gives me the shivers." Betty gasped. As we progressed upward, the creek became smaller and smaller, until it was just a tiny branch. Since we had shed our gear and were traveling much lighter, we came out on top by twelve o'clock. Surprisingly, the top of the pass was fairly flat, so we decided to eat lunch – just some canned sausages and crackers. Buck ate the same.

We didn't tarry long, for the going would be much more difficult. The view from here was spectacular. Betty wanted to linger to drink it all in, but I insisted that we be on our way.

The going downhill was steep and we had to take great care not to stumble and fall. Sometimes, it's easier to climb than to go down a steep mountain. Finally, the wire fence corner came into view, and reaching it, we turned west and followed for what seemed like ages. The low, rock shelf to our left also extended along the fence line. At last, we reached the small waterfall, where I had first discovered the garnets.

Betty was all for searching the pool, right away, she was so excited. Right away, she found a stone and began scraping in the sandy pool, finding garnets, with almost every scrape. I used the small folding spade in the sandy soil, off from the pool, and the stones were plentiful. Each spade full, washed in the water, would reveal several stones.

I paused, looked at my watch, and told Betty it was time to leave; by now, we had a small sack full of stones and they were almost too heavy to carry with one hand. Reluctantly, Betty agreed, and we left for the Overhang.

Reaching the wire corner, we turned upward, toward the top and where the pass began. This was the roughest part of the trip; for the mountain slope was at least sixty degrees. At times, progress was made only by grasping saplings or anything that a hand might hold onto. Resting frequently, it took us an hour to reach the top.

There, we were forced to rest and now the sun was behind the mountain peak to our right. Without sunlight, the pass would grow increasingly darker, the further down we descended. No time to linger, we started down at a rapid stride and the mile long pass was quickly left behind, some thirty minutes later. Turning right on the Indian trail, the going was easier and a few minutes later, the Overhang was reached.

The sun was barely hanging in the sky and I went to work immediately, starting a fire. Betty pitched in and brought in more wood that was cut this morning. Piling three six foot logs together, I elevated one end and built a fire with small pieces of wood underneath. Once the logs began to burn, they would last at least until midnight; then I would have to get up and pile more wood on it.

Our job with the fire and the wood finished, Betty began to prepare supper, while I spread the sleeping bags next to the Overhang wall. We would sleep between the wall and the fire, since the heat would also reflect off the wall. While we were busy, Buck had wondered off and was barking some distance away. "Well, I know where he is; he's at that damned ground hog hole again." "I'll have to go get him." I stormed.

Buck was some two hundred yards from camp and at the same hole as before; scolding, I yanked him by the collar and half pulled him away. What meager food Betty was able to scrounge, we ate with relish, but she promised to make up for it when we got back to the Norton house.

After supper, we sat on some logs, the only sound, was the crackling of the fire. Soon, some owls, far below, began their early nightly hooting. "I can't see how they find something to eat, if they keep that frightening noise up." Betty declared. "Maybe they get together and plan their hunt, like wolves, with their howling." I answered. We got into out sleeping bags and Betty was intrigued with the firelight dancing off the ceiling. "Reminds me of Indians, dancing around the fire." She said. We slept more comfortably on the soft earth than last night on the Norton floor. I got up only once during the night to replenish the fire and its warmth kept us comfortable, despite the bitter cold, some few yards away.

We arose at dawn, the fire, still burning, would be allowed to slowly die; but if it wasn't out by the time we left, we would have to shovel dirt to smother it. One had to be extremely cautious; a forest fire up here would be disastrous! Betty fixed what could be described as "breakfast"; we ate, sharing it with Buck.

Rolling up the sleeping bags and packing the rest of the gear, we selected a diagonal descending course and struck out down the mountain. Within some thirty minutes, the top of the long white oak ridge was reached. Now, the going was much smoother; the long ridge was a haven for all manner of game and the seed fall had been excellent. I would probably come back and hunt it this afternoon. Another half hour and we were in the orchard. Frozen apples under the leaves were everywhere; evidence of animals, feeding on them, indicated that this also would be a likely place to hunt! Passing on through the orchard, the Norton house was reached, shortly.

Harvest Time

It was late morning and Betty prepared a meal, which compensated for the scrimpy food that we endured on the mountain. Since this would be the last day and the drive back to Cashiers before dark would be necessary, both of us planned to hunt immediately. When one is hunting, the thrill, the exhilaration, overcomes any previous fatigue, such as the tiresome trip on the mountain; I was alert, expectant!

Betty planned to hunt in the middle of the orchard, so I struck out for the white oak ridge. Since the air slowly drained upward, my scent would not be detected from below.

Entering the woods from the orchard, I eased my way upward, a considerable distance, and took up a position at the foot of a large oak. Facing downward and towards the west, the view was excellent. As things quieted down, squirrels began to run to and froe, searching for acorns; then grouse passed close by on the way to the orchard.

I had sat for an hour and was about to move to another section of the ridge, when suddenly, two deer appeared off to the right. They were below me and would not catch my scent. Closer they came; a spike buck and a doe, following close behind. Within shotgun range now, I leveled on the bucks' lower neck, as both the deer were facing me head on. As I pulled the right barrel, both deer went down; then the doe got up and staggered to the side. I had not meant to kill her, but the buckshot, evidently, had swept to the side of the first deer and wounded her, badly. There was nothing to do, but finish her off. Now, I had some grueling work on my hands!

Field dressing the deer took me some thirty minutes or more, and my hands were bloody and slimy, with no water to clean them. Finishing the dressing, I tied the rear feet together with a short piece of rope that I kept for such purposes, then began dragging them down the mountain. Try dragging two deer with one hand while holding a shot gun with the other! "this isn't going to work." I told myself. "My arm is being pulled out of it's socket." Fortunately, the rope binding the deer was long enough to cut in half to make a sling for the gun and to still bind the feet. The system wasn't the most comfortable, but at least two hands were better pulling the carcasses.

I was just approaching the top of the orchard when three shots rang out below. Boom, boom – then boom. Well, I don't think that's a danger signal; at least, the shots were not evenly spaced. I had taught Betty the danger signal – three evenly timed shots. Ten minutes later, Betty and Buck were waiting for me at the side of the orchard.

"What's all that shooting about?" I asked. "Sounded like a war going on!" She held up two grouse, proudly waving them in my face. "Honey, by the time you get those deer skinned and dressed, we can't possibly go back to Cahiers today." "Well, that's what I figured." I answered. By the time that we reached the Norton place, my arms were numb, their sockets, seemingly, void of rotor cups.

Betty was right; from the time that she helped me swing the first deer, until the second one was skinned and quartered, it was too late to even think about returning to Cashiers, that day.

Utterly pooped, I did manage to build a fire in the kitchen range and finally got some feeling back into my numbed hands. While Betty prepared one of the grouse for supper, I sat by the stove and enjoyed every sip of Jack Daniels, before downing it. I watched her prepare the bird; first she parboiled it a few minutes, then stuffing it with corn bread crumbs, sage and minced onions; she placed it in the oven. Checking it in twenty minutes, she pulled it from the oven; it was golden brown; what a scene – what a woman! We dined on baked grouse and apple pie for desert.

That night, sleeping on the hard floor was hardly noticeable, since both of us were so tired after the mountaintop and after fooling with the deer.

We got an early start next morning and were in Cashiers by 9 o'clock. After unpacking, I went down to the general store and bought a sausage grinder and some wrapping paper. The meat was sectioned into roasts, steaks and ground hamburger. Some of the hamburger, I mixed with seasoned pork sausage; this would make it more lean and healthier for us.

The next job around the store was absolutely essential, and hopefully, the last, was to build a lean-to shelter attached to the store side. The vehicles simply had to be protected from the weather. Bumgarner had plenty of construction grade hemlock lumber. Next morning, I drove to Sylva and ordered enough galvanized sheets of roofing, that were promised in the afternoon. Returning, I spent the balance of the day digging holes for posts. The shed was to be 20 feet by 24 feet, enough to house both vehicles. When the materials came, I had to build a ladder first, before the rafters could be placed. With Betty's help, we completed the work in four days. Completing the job, I said, "Now, Honey, we can relax for the rest of the winter." "That's a joke!, You'll always be finding something to work on." She retorted. "Honey, as I was processing the meat, I was thinking that we aught to buy a regular freezer, because the refrig freezer is filled up. A couple of hundred pounds of meat would last most of the year; think of how much money we could save!" Pondering this, she agreed. "Let's go to Ashville and look for one; you also wanted some tools to make jewelry; we could look for that, too."

On Saturday, we drove by Sylva, but the appliance store there only had a small freezer. An hour later, we left Buck in the car and searched for some appliance stores in Ashville. We chose a store that sold General Electric brands.

After explaining to the clerk that we needed a freezer that would hold two hundred pounds, he advised to get one with at least twenty cubic feet. "Well, we live in Cashiers, do you deliver that far?" "Yes, we would, but that will cost you fifty dollars, extra." The freezer was $175, and delivery, $50. "I can deliver it sometime Monday." The clerk promised.

Next we inquired around and found a surplus Army store. I bought two canvas folding cots and some rope with a block and tackle. We could easily swing deer or other heavy game with ease.

Our next quest was to find a hobby store, so we walked along McDowell Street until we found a jewelry store. "Maybe they'll know where to look, let's go in." Betty urged.

A smiling, dark complexioned man approached and asked, "What can I help you with?" Betty exclaimed that we were looking for a hobby store that sold jewelry making things. Thinking for a minute, the man gave us directions. "May I ask what kinds of jewelry will you be working with?" He said. "I have some garnets; she reached into her pocket book and showed him several, handing him one. Holding it to the light, he studied it for several moments, turning it this way and that. Finally he asked, "Where did you get this?" I looked at Betty sharply; she caught my eye. "Why, I got them from an old Indian, he wouldn't tell me where he had gotten them." "Would you sell me what you have there in your hand?" "Well, sir, I don't know what they would be worth, I only know what I paid for them." Betty fibbed. "Well, mam, if I may ask, what did you pay for them?" "I paid a dollar a piece for them." Betty, again, fibbed. "Would you take $2 a piece for them?" Betty replied, "Let's see." She counted what she had, "I have ten here. I'll let you have five." The man paid her then asked for her name and address.

Following the jeweler's directions, we found a hobby shop in the next block. "Yes, we have a large selection of jewelry making equipment. You know that North Carolina is famous for producing almost every kind of precious stones." "Many people come in wanting to buy this type of equipment." The clerk showed Betty a large section of the store devoted entirely to jewelry making hobby. She selected several styles of sterling silver chain, sterling silver clips, snaps, etc. I need a soldering iron and silver solder. A small electric saw and grinder caught her attention; she studied it longingly, then looked at me with pleading eyes. "For God's sake honey, buy the thing." I demanded. We finished and went to the car.

Poor Buck. I knew he needed a comfort stop, so we drove out to a large warehouse and let him out.

We drove back up town and parked near Park Square, hoping to find a nearby restaurant. Strolling up the square, we stopped at the World War I German cannon. Patting the barrel, I said, "It has a personal history behind it." "Personal history, what kind of personal history?" Betty wanted to know. "My father was seriously wounded when trying to capture this cannon: several of his men were wounded and killed." (Note: the cannon was captured by Company I, 321st Infantry, 81st Division, First sergeant, Robert G. Edney.) "You know, the French would not allow the Americans to ship this cannon out of France, so my father's unit simply disassembled it, crated it up, and labeled it "Property of the United Sates" and sent it to Ashville!

We found a restaurant, ordered, and enjoyed someone else's cooking. Reaching home late that evening, Betty was so elated over her jewelry making paraphernalia, that she spread the whole works on the kitchen table, marveling over each piece! As we had eaten lunch, Betty finally put away her toys and fixed a light meal for supper.

Monday at 10 o'clock, the freezer was delivered. "Well, it's empty." I said. "Won't do any good empty; what say we pack up the Jeep and head for the Norton place; we need to store in a supply of meat?' "Well, I'm with you honey, but let's take plenty of food and don't forget the cots." Betty agreed.

We were well packed and on our way within an hour's time, arriving at the Norton place forty-five minutes later. Unpacking and fixing a quick lunch, we set out to hunt; it was now early afternoon. I had seen lots of hog signs on the white oak ridge and this is where I was headed for. Since a hog can wind you, as well as, deer or bear, I needed to get far up on the ridge and then begin hunting back down. This way, currents and scents drifting up the mountain would be in my favor. Betty would hunt her favorite spot, in the orchard.

Reaching the top of the ridge, I waited a half hour or so, then began easing back down. Seeing, nor hearing nothing, I crept on, then stopped, suddenly. Some kind of loud ruckus was taking place below, squealing and bawling. I rushed down and a sight to behold! A large sow was attacking a half grown bear. The bear, own it's back was attempting to regain it's feet and flee, under the onslaughts of the sow. Young pigs were running around in circles, apparently so confused

34

they couldn't decide whether to stay with their mother or run away. I leveled at two of the largest and dropped them with both barrels. At the blast of the gun, every animal left the vicinity in a wild, grunting confusion!

Quickly, reloading the gun, in case the sow recovered her wits and came back, looking for her offspring, I began to field dress the shoats. They had fattened all summer on apples and later in the fall, on immense crop of acorns. Now, they were up to almost a hundred pounds. This time, I remembered to equip my gun with a sling.

Field dressing took a long time and the trip down, dragging the hogs would be slow indeed! The dressing finished, the hind feet were tied together and with a short rope, I could drag them with some effort.

Wild Hogs

Betty fired two shots from below as I was preparing to leave. "Must be a grouse, or turkey." I surmised. The pigs felt like lead, forcing me to stop frequently to rest. A half hour later, I whistled sharply as I entered the orchard. Betty answered from below. Reaching her, finally, I asked what the shooting was about, since she didn't hold up a grouse, pointing to the side, she said, "There." A large doe lay there to be field dressed. Now, we had a mess on our hands!

I immediately began field dressing the deer for it was getting up in the late afternoon. Betty wouldn't be able to drag the deer, even though it was gutted. I would have to come back later for it.

She carried the guns and I continued down with the two pigs. When we reached the house, I immediately started back up for the deer. With Buck following, we reached it in twenty minutes. Tying both rear feet together, I began the journey back down. Needless to say, I was exhausted when finally I reached the house. After a long rest, Betty helped me to swing the two pigs high enough so that a bear or bobcat couldn't reach them. The deer were placed in an old wagon bed.

I managed to start a fire in the kitchen range and sat by it, so exhausted, I could hardly move. Betty handed me a nice drink of my favorite, and after two slow swigs, life returned within me. Betty prepared deer liver and onions, smothered in gravy for supper.

We sat around the kitchen table, completely relaxed, after a fine meal and a couple of drinks. Betty was concerned about the orchard, the trees were old-fashioned kind. If the orchard were left alone, it would be completely swallowed up by the white pine and hardwood trees. "We cannot allow that. Elbert suggested I go see Frank Holden and see if he would allow his son to clear the orchard with a bulldozer." "Well, if we expect to make this our home, it's got to be fixed up." Betty said. "I would like to put an addition onto the house; this could be made of white pine logs and a large rock fireplace at the end of it, would be nice. Most all the materials are right here on the property and it wouldn't cost us much." I pointed out.

We sat up the canvas cots, spread our sleeping bags and retired. Buck, poor fellow, had to sleep on an old quilt. The cots were a vast improvement over the hard floor, at least the night passed more smoothly than before!

Next day, I worked on the carcasses until almost noon. Finally, packing everything in the Jeep, we left for Cashiers.

If I were to do most of the work on the Norton addition, winter would prevent any work except maybe hauling rock to the building site for the fireplace. During the mild days in winter, if there were any, I could take the Jeep and a trailer and keep busy. I had noticed a large number of junked cars behind Mike Bryson's station. Perhaps, he could take the rear end of a junked Model A Ford and make a small trailer.

As Buck and I walked down towards the service station, I noticed an old rusty steam engine in the woods, probably once used to pull a sawmill, I surmised. Anyway, it would make a nice tourist attraction, if cleaned up and painted a bright color. I'll see what Betty thinks about it, I promised myself.

Mike was servicing a 1938 Ford sedan as we walked up. Since the tourist season was well past, he was very interested when I broached the subject of a trailer. "Yes, it would be simple to take the rear end of a Model A Ford and make a trailer, in fact, since work is slack, I can start it, anytime.

The problem with the orchard kept gnawing away at me. At least a large section of it could be salvaged, if work were started soon enough. Unlike many commercial orchards, the trees here were of the old-fashioned kind and many dated back to the 1700's. Species such as Roxbury, Black Twigg, Arkansas Blacks, old-fashioned Red Winesap, Red June and many, many others. Surely, Holden with his heavy equipment, could clean the orchard in short order. Elbert had advised the best time to find Holden at home would be Sunday afternoon.

The following Sunday afternoon, Betty and I drove to Glenville; a clear, cold afternoon would find most people comfortably sitting around a fireplace and perhaps dozing after a large Sunday dinner. Such was the case when we were introduced and invited in.

As we took chairs around a huge fireplace, Bessie Holden asked what branch of the Butler family were we related to. "Well, my great aunt was Elizabeth Butler Moss and we used to visit her in the 1920's." I answered. "She was my Mother." Bessie said. "And welcome to the family."

The Holden's had three sons, twins and Tommy, the youngest. Frank ran heavy equipment, building roads, grading and sometime logging. He agreed to put Tommy on the orchard the coming Tuesday morning. "As long as the snow isn't too deep, he can work." Frank said.

Monday morning after breakfast, I dropped by Mike's Service Station to pick up the trailer. After some minor adjustment to hook it to the Jeep, I drove it home; if I didn't overload it, it should be fine for hauling the stone. Betty and I discussed whether or not to spend the time at the Norton place while Holden worked in the orchard; we finally decided it best to be there just in case we were needed for an emergency. Packing enough food and supplies to last several days, we left for there early Tuesday morning. Holden was already there, unloading his equipment. While Betty resumed cleaning the Norton house, I began hauling stone from the old pasture.

Tommy had brought in a D-6 dozer with a shear blade and also would use a heavy bush hog later. He decided to start at the top and push down the hill, thus, clearing between the trees. When this was finished, he would clear the blocks that remained between the rows, running parallel to the contour.

For the balance of the week, the weather continued to cooperate, with sunny days and mild temperatures, allowing Holden to complete the job by Saturday afternoon. Before moving the equipment, I had Tommy to push a road leading to the bottom creek. This would allow me to haul sand from the creek. Also, Tommy agreed to come back in the late spring and skid the white pine logs for the building.

Throughout the winter months, I kept busy on fair days, hauling stone and sand, and pruning the apple orchard. Betty was content in designing and making jewelry from the garnets and sterling. Her problem was now that she was running short of the garnets. Ice and snow on the high elevations would make it next to impossible for me to go up and get more for her. Also, the jeweler in Ashville kept after her for more garnets. It would be mid April before I could get up there.

While waiting for the snow to melt on the mountain, I busied with laying the foundation of the new addition and started the rock work for the fireplace. I especially enjoyed doing the rock work for the fireplace, but could only go so high with it until the logs were put in place. After the foundation was finished, I ordered the sills and rafters from Elbert's mill. When the lumber was delivered, I carefully measured and cut the rafters.

Just west of the old pasture, a thirty year old stand of white pine was large enough for the logs. Diameters at breast high, measured up to fourteen inches or better and since the building would measure thirty by forty feet, I cut the straightest trees, free of limbs that could be found. The walls of the building were to be around ten feet high on the foundation, so I figured that some fifty trees would suffice.

As spring crept slowly up the mountainside, it's presence announced by untold millions of wildflowers, animal life also joined nature's emergence. Turkey gobblers roamed the ridges, displaying their iridescence colors, in hopes of attracting a female,; grouse drumming on a weathered chestnut log, announcing their presence; ravens, perched on dead snags atop high cliffs, seemingly fussing with each other; yes, nature's chorus was highly vocal, announcing spring's approach!

For the past five months, he had slept fitfully, occasionally turning this way or that, perhaps seeking a more comfortable position, or was it the pains of hunger in his stomach, that began to awaken him? After all, it had been some five months since his last meal, but whatever it was, it was now urging him to go forth and search for food. His craving was not for a mere squirrel, but something more juicy, far more filling; he knew exactly what that was and where to find it.

Emerging from the cave after the long winter required some length of time to once again regain his senses of survival. Slowly, poking a huge triangular head partly through the narrow opening, his forked tongue now began to assemble and extrapolate the molecules of air drifting up.

As the sparse sunrays began to warm his blood, his movements now became more precise and sure. Emerging fully from his den, he headed downward to the long white oak ridge. Fighting the temptation of an easy squirrel, for nothing would take the place of his intended meal, he pressed on.

Arriving at the ridge in late morning was not the ideal time to hunt, for most of the game had fed much earlier and now rested until it would again feed in the afternoon. Meantime then, the Keeper had plenty of time to spend a fitfully early afternoon, searching for an ideal spot to prepare for his meal.

Selecting a position under a sloping rock formation, which lay next to a well-worn game trail, he dozed, perhaps dreaming of a juicy young piglet. It wasn't easy though, with those hunger pains gnawing at his gut.

The big sow, with a litter of recent born piglets moved up the ridge, following a well trodden game trail, which would eventually lead her to a cliff, where she usually bedded down for the night. She had spent the middle of the day, up to mid afternoon, down below in a cool, shaded hollow, where the brood could wallow in a branch. Now, an afternoon meal of last fall's acorns, although scarce, would top off today's meal.

Her litter was yet too small to root for food, so they spent their time chasing each other, or staging mock fights, however, they always stayed behind her, as she searched for dangers ahead.

Suddenly, the big snake was jolted out of his doze, the forked tongue never to be caught off guard, had warned of the potential food – or danger, coming up from below. His vision was limited, for unlike most creatures, his view was only effective for a few short feet. The forked tongue however, could detect any source of food or danger over great distance, depending, of course, on the direction of the air currents.

Stiffening as he recognized the sow, for she was not only a deadly enemy, but also a source of his favorite food, he flattened close to the ground.

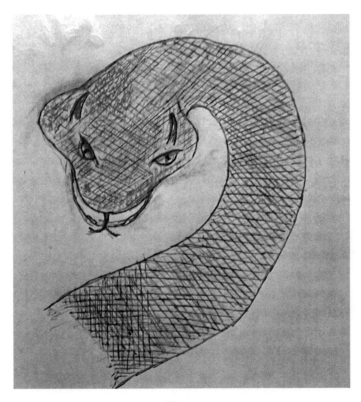

Keeper

The sow passed close to his hiding place, but failed to detect any scent, since the air currents were moving uphill with her.

The young pigs spread out, like a covey of quail, followed somewhat behind, not able to detect any danger. Selecting a hindmost individual, the snake struck with a lightening speed; his great mouth clamping over the unfortunate creature's snout. It could neither breathe nor utter a sound, as it was snatched underneath the rock ledge. In less than three minutes, it's struggles ceased and now the great serpent began his meal. After the meal, the snake would return to the mountain, not to his winter den, but up the pass, under a huge boulder. Here it would be cool and small game , passing just a few feet away, would offer easy pickings.

After Tommy Holden had finished skidding the logs to the building site, my work in earnest now began. True, skinning the bark on any species of logs isn't easily done, but white pine is probably more difficult than most. This, no doubt, is due to the resin in the bark and also the hidden knots. This work is always done by hand in springtime when the sap rises. The tool for this work is a bark spud, a curved small spade-like tool.

Probably some of the hardest work that I have ever done is "spudding" the bark from white pine logs. I worked a full week stripping the logs. Now, I needed two days of rest.

Betty wanted to try her hand at trout fishing, but we had no fishing gear. "Well, let's go to Sylva and buy some fly rods and stuff." She suggested. Jackson County is famous for it's trout fishing, surely, they sell such stuff there."

Sure enough, a large hardware store handled not only trout gear, but almost any other type of sporting goods materials. We bought two cheap fly rods, line and reels, and some inexpensive flys.

Late that afternoon, we walked down to the lower stream, with no waders or tall rubber boots, we would have to cast from the bank. Selecting a sand bar to stand on, I showed Betty how to make a slow, easy cast, and as the fly swirled in a half circle, the rod tip bent almost double as a large trout hit the fly. Handing the rod to my squealing wife, I stood back and watched her fight the fish, leading it to a sandbar, she held it up and glossed over it's beauty.

We moved upstream, so as not to disturb any lurking trout, and found another open spot to cast from. This time, Betty made the cast, winding up to make a huge effort, then – zipp!, her fly was snagged in an alder bush behind her. She exploded some sort of expletive, which I failed to understand. I soothed her feelings by retrieving the fly and with a short cast, another fish was on. We fished for a couple of hours, releasing all but a half dozen for supper.

At supper that evening, we enjoyed crispy rainbow trout, cold slaw and hush puppies. Buck, not to be left out, also delighted in the meal.

"Bob, I have just got to have more garnets; it's the middle of tourist season and we depend on that to pay our taxes and food bills. I realize that you've worked hard on the logs, but maybe you can bring enough stones back this time to last for the season." "Well honey, you're the breadwinner, I'll leave in the morning. You realize, of course, that I'll have to spend a couple nights at the overhang." "In that case, I'll take some supplies as far as the overhang for you, then come back there later to help you." Betty suggested.

The joys of a beautiful meal that evening and leisurely tomorrow were now dashed, knowing what an excruciating next two days lay in store for me that night. I dreamt of hard climbs over never ending rock slides, which seemed to appear again and again.

Nevertheless, we were up early the next morning and after a heavy breakfast, were on the way to the Overhang. There, Betty would leave her burden of supplies and she and Buck would return to the Norton House. She had insisted on my taking Buck with me but I would have nothing of it. I simply told her that my mind would be on her safety if he went with me. Finally, she relented and took the big dog with her.

We reached the Overhang by nine thirty. I kissed my wife and continued on the way to the garnet location. Nearing the huge boulders in the pass, I got a whiff of rattlesnake and skirted the boulders, because at that point, was very close to the rocks.

Hurrying on upward, I noticed that remnants of spring still lingered as I neared the top. Pausing only a few minutes to catch my breath, the way downward would be a bit easier, if I could keep my feet under me.

Turning left at the wire fence corner, the waterfalls appeared in short order. Here, I lost no time, casting the pack aside, I took the spade and began to dig in the sandy soil. With each spadeful, I dissolved it in the small pool and extracted the garnets, as they were exposed in the bright sunlight. Although there was a large area of unworked soil remaining, I noticed that the chunks of rock around me seemed to contain some of the larger garnets. These, apparently had fallen from the seam above. After filing a sack of the loose gems, I chose a twenty pound rock that showed many garnets, embedded in its' sides. Placing the sack of loose stones in the pack, I shouldered this, and could now use both hands free to carry the loose chunk of embedded rock.

Early afternoon approaching, and with a heavy burden, it would be a torturous trip back to the Overhang. Forced to rest several times, I reached the top of the pass at last, and simply fell to the ground to rest. The rest of the trip from here would be downhill.

The short rest revived me and I started the long decent down the pass, discretely, circling the boulders as I came near them. Struggling on with the load, the Overhang was welcomed relief at last. It was nearing sundown now and starting a fire, and rummaging in the pack of food that Betty had deposited, a bottle of Jack Daniels appeared. Now, for the first time this day, I could savor a few sips and relax.

As I ate the sparse meal and enjoyed the drink, my mind kept wondering about the odor of snake around the great boulders. Why would a snake hang around such a place? Whatever the reason, it would be wise to keep my distance from this place.

As darkness crept in, the temperature began to plummet, for at this altitude, despite warm May, a good fire for the night would keep me comfortable. Sleep came easily, for every fiber in my body seemed to cry out for relief.

Rising as soon as it was light enough for me to see, I ate hurriedly and was on the way back to the garnets. Betty would meet me this afternoon at the Overhang to help with the carrying the loads back to the Norton house.

The pass was chilly in the twilight, for the sun would only reach its bottom later in the morning. Once again, I skirted the boulders and continued upward. What a forlorn, ghostly, lonely place the pass at this time of day! I reached the falls by nine thirty. Today, I would find a nice chunk of garnet embedded rock, and not waste any time with digging for loose stones. Selecting, what I figured was a twelve or fourteen pound such stone was easy. Stooping down to get a drink of water, something greenish caught my eye. I picked up a broken, six sided piece of stone, opaque in color. "Now, where did this come from?" I wondered. Searching the area hurriedly, I could find no more and reasoned that it might have washed down a small stream.

Struggling up the tiny branch, at times having to grab hold of rocks or sparse growth to help me, I followed the stream. Finally, I came face to face with the shear bare faced mountain wall itself, and could go no further.

A whitish, circular area in the granite wall stood out in sharp contrast to the darker background. Large chunks of the light material lay around, evidently, they had broken loose from the parent material many years ago. Searching these, I found a large chunk, with a perfect tubular stone, the same color as the broken one, embedded in rock. This would make a nice knife handle, I reasoned, so I decided to take it along. The chunk probably weighed close to twenty pounds, but I was excited and determined to carry it with me. Betty's chunk of twelve pound garnet rock, I could carry in the shoulder pack, so I could handle the new found rock with both hands.

Working along the side of the steep mountain towards the steep upward trail was a struggle, indeed! At times, I had to drop the chunk of rock and hold on to a sapling to keep from falling down the mountain. Reaching the upward trail was little relief, it being steeply upward. The top, as it was yesterday, now was a place to rest. If I were to meet Betty at the Overhang, a rest now was out of the question. Somehow, I managed to start the downward trek and continue on. Nearing the large boulders, I again, gave them a wide berth. At two o'clock sharp, the Overhang, and Betty, came into view. Barks and kisses were my rewards!

"Folks, this is nice, but we have to reach the Norton house before sundown!" I cautioned. But now, there was a twenty pound sack of loose garnets and three chunks of matrix rock to carry, what to do" Thinking for a moment, "I'll do it Indian style." I said. Selecting some small spruce saplings, I formed an "A" frame, then taking my short jacket, ran the two legs of the frame up the sleeves of the jacket. Securing these, I now had a cradle for the rocks; this would be much easier to pull, than to try to carry! We made the Norton house just before sundown.

Fortunately, Betty had prepared a meal beforehand, and all she had to do was to heat it up. It was such a relief that night just to sleep in a canvass cot!

Back in Cashiers the next day, I placed the three chunks of rock on the store's shelf and forgot about them; they had been such a nightmare for me to handle! Now, Betty could work for a long time with the twenty pound bag of loose garnets.

"As soon as I notch the logs, Holden is going to bring over a front end loader with forks to erect the building, also, he's got two men to help with placing the logs." I told Betty. "I'll go over tomorrow and start the axe work." "Well, you take Buck with you in case you get cut or something happens." Betty insisted. "No." I protested. "You keep Buck; you know all kinds of tourists are on the roads these days and I'd feel much more at ease with Buck near you." Finally, Betty gave in and agreed with me. "I can work five or six hours a day and come home at night. I'll be fine."

The logs had to be notched at the exact spot so they would fit snugly together. The cuts were made, starting exactly eight inches from each end of the log. Using a Kelly, three and a half pound axe, that was kept sharp as a razor, the work proceeded as I had planned. As each log was notched on top, I turned it over with a cant hook and notched the other side. At noon, I ate the sandwich that my wife had made for me and this was washed down by hot coffee I made on the Norton kitchen stove. Nevertheless, it took two full days of hard work to finish the logs. While sitting around at lunch time, I wondered about the roof. What was I to do about that?

There were plenty of nice red oaks on the property, and these were used almost always for shingles. But, winter, when the sap was down, was the best time to rive them and I didn't exactly know how to do this, and it would also require lots of time.

When I had worked in Wilmington, I remembered that sawmills in Pender County sawed shingles out of Juniper or White Cedar. This wood, although softer than oak, nevertheless, was very durable. They even made boats out of it. Perhaps this would be the way to go, then. I decided to look into it.

Betty had made only five bracelets and two necklaces from the garnets in two days and sold none. "If you sell the garnets to the jeweler in Ashville, at least you would have a market for them; at least you wouldn't have to work so hard. Just setting there for hours, all stooped over, isn't good for you." I pointed out. "I know, but let me try for a couple of weeks, maybe business will pick up, if it doesn't, then we can let the jeweler have the stones."

Tommy Holden was to show up on Tuesday to start on the building and when the day arrived, he was there on time. His machine was a Cat #9-55, front end loader. With forks, he could lift a load, twelve feet high off the ground. The two helpers were stationed on each end of the logs to guide then into the notches of the bottom logs.

Betty and I watched, fascinated, as the men worked with clockwork precision, as the logs began to form the building. At first, the work proceeded with great speed, but as the building got higher, the men on each end had to use poles, with spikes on the ends to guide the logs in place. After the logs were erected, cross beams were placed on top. Next, the precut rafters were lifted and deposited on top of the cross beams, this would save me lots of hard work. Lastly, Holden lifted a small pile of boards on top; these would serve as a scaffold, or platform, to stand on when the rafters were erected.

CHAPTER III

George Owl

"At this point, it looks as if things are set right for me to start working on the upper part of the building." Thinking about the Norton place, I told Betty. "Someone should be there with me in case of an accident." "Frankly, I'm not fond of you working on top of that building, can't you just wait until we can hire somebody to help you? You know that I've got to keep after the jewelry business until the tourist season is over." "Well then," I answered, "suppose we divide the week up, say, both of us spend Monday through Thursday over there and the rest of the week here in Cashiers?" "Why the rush to finish the Norton place; it's not making us any money; at least this meager tourist business is. All that rock pile of a mountain we bought has been nothing but an expense. Yes, I suppose we can divide the week up and try to work that way." Betty resignedly gave in.

On Monday, we were at the Norton place by eight o'clock: I wanted to get some work done before the hot June mid-day set in. Betty busied with things in the house, while Buck, up to his usual, roamed the area, poking his nose into anything that looked appealing.

The first job on top was to nail a walkway along each side and run one running through the center; hence, I would have a platform to stand on while erecting the rafters. Since the rise of the roof above center was to be six feet, then, how could one man, working alone, bring two heavy rafters together and nail them? With a few minutes, pondering the situation, the solution was to build a support in the center to hold the rafters while I could nail them.

By the time that the two rafters were nailed together, forming a completed roof truss, it was nearing noontime, an occasional whiff from the kitchen reminded me!

Betty had made us a stew from last winters frozen deer meat and the accompanying vegetables, it was a gourmet's delight. So much so, that I decided to take a nap afterwards.

It was still so hot that I decided to just call it a day and relax. Late afternoon, we walked out to the road and sat on the bridge, then Betty took her fly rod and practiced casting, catching many small mountain trout, which she gingerly released. As the sun was beginning to sink in the western sky, we headed back towards the house; several deer bounded across the road ahead of us, waving their white flags, perhaps taunting us, as they rapidly disappeared.

Early next morning, my plan was to get some work accomplished before the heat became offensive. Breakfast over, the second set of rafters, first had to be muscled into place. This was not an easy task while balancing yourself on a narrow walkway. Once the first rafter was in place, then it was nailed at it's bottom, then the opposing rafter from the other side was joined in the middle at the top. I was ready to turn to the third set of rafters, when Betty called from below.

"Bob, we have a visitor and he wants to talk to you." Glancing down, I saw a rather large man standing near the foot of the ladder. "Oh, boy! I thought, here I am treed like a possum, without a weapon. Glancing towards Betty, she smiled reassuringly, patting her apron, for I knew underneath that apron was a 9mm Browning automatic and she certainly knew how to use it. Descending the ladder, I stopped on the first rung to face the man, eyeball to eyeball. A rather large man, dark skin, straight hair, slightly graying at the temples and dark piercing eyes. Has to be a full blood Cherokee, I was thinking. Extending a large hand with a vice-like grip, he introduced himself as George Owl, from over about Whiteside Mountain. As we shook, I suggested that we move over to a lumber pile in the shade, where we could talk.

Opening the conversations, I asked, "Now, where have I heard your name before, of course, from my father. He spoke of a George Owl in his company of World War One." Owl looked at me and then said, "81st Division, 321 Infantry, Company I." "So, you are that George Owl." I answered with amazement. "Yes, your father was my first sergeant and he also recommended me for sergeant." George said.

"Well, George, welcome to the Butler Family and I want you to know that you can hunt over here anytime you please.

At first, Buck was somewhat standoffish and kept his distance, but I suppose that he somehow sensed from out conversation, was friendly and eventually, came over and sat between us." Now, Buck, shake hands with George like a good boy." I demanded. Buck extended a huge paw and George shook it, with amazement.

Betty emerged from the house carrying a large pitcher of lemonade, which she poured for us. "So, George, I assume that you have hunted many times on this mountain before?" "Yes, when the Norton's were here, my father and grandfather brought me to hunt here from time to time. I was probably six or seven years old. You know, every time I go on this mountain, I find something new; it's a big mountain, full of mysteries." Not intending to be over inquisitive, I did want to know more about George and his family, so I approached the subject as gingerly as possible. "Yes, I had a family once, but my son was killed in WWII and my wife passed away three years ago. I do have two nephews over at Cherokee that I'm close to. They are policemen on the reservation. They have also hunted with me here." "Of course, I would like to help you with work on the house, or other work around this place." "That's nice of you George, but we can't afford to pay you since our only source of income is what my wife makes on the jewelry business during tourist season." "I wouldn't think of expecting pay from you, since you have offered to let me hunt on this property, I could bring a canvass cot over and sleep in the barn while working here." "There is plenty of room in this house, just bring your cot and sleep in the house; you can take your meals with us when you're here. When we're not here, you can use the kitchen just like you do at home." "That sounds great, I'll go home and get my cot and some stuff and comeback tomorrow."

The following morning, George showed up early and we made rapid progress on the rafters. When two people are working on a project the job goes much faster in all respects, than a single person can accomplish. We finished the roof trusses in two days. Now I had to call Fred Barnes and have him arrange to send me a load of white cedar shingles for the roof. Also, I wanted the flooring to be quarter-sawn longleaf pine.

As the weather grew warmer in July, the tourist business increased for Betty and we could only spend three days a week at the Norton place. People living in the coastal plains of the Carolinas and Georgia were seeking relief from the hot, humid climate and many passed through Cashers, which added to Betty's jewelry business.

When working on the Norton addition, we would listen to George spin stories about the Cherokees and his hunting experiences. One night after supper and when we were having a few drinks, George suddenly reached in a hind pocket and pulled out a small leather pouch. Opening it, he pulled out a beautiful green crystal. A small hole had been drilled through the end of the piece and a thin leather string passed through, forming a necklace. Holding it up for my inspection, I immediately identified at as a large emerald. It must have been worth a huge fortune! "Where did you get it?" I asked, trying to sound as casual as possible. "From up there." George said, with a wide sweep of his hands towards the mountain. "You mean, my mountain?" "Yes, your mountain – from a cave, the old ones told me, but we have searched for a cave over many years and never found one. My grandfather, my father and me, we searched and searched over every foot of that mountain! I think this thing might have been traded from the South American Indians and maybe brought up through Mexico. You know, I studied about such things in college." George was empathetic. "Anyway, you know how we Cherokees are, we set around a campfire and spend stories, some of these may be based on fact, but I guess most are just stories that are made up."

The next day, we had to leave for Cashiers. Stopping by Mike's Service Station, I placed a call to Fred for the shingles and asked him to saw some quality pine for the floor. By this time, Fred Barnes had built up a good lumber business based on pine and cypress. When buying tracts of timber with some hardwood on it, he would log the hardwood and sell it to other mills. The hardwood mills in turn, would sell Fred pine and cypress logs. With an efficient mill crew, Fred could spend more time on the telephone, selling his lumber or finding tracts of timber. The area around Wilmington was a good source for timber, but yet there was also a lot of competition for this wood. After all, the Atlantic Ocean was right next door and the mills had only a half circle to procure their timber in. Fred was concerned about the future for his mill, with the competition being what it is. Fred had pleaded with me to go into business with him, since I was trained as a forester with lots of experience. This is when we both worked together in Wilmington.

As promised, the white cedar shingles arrived in a weeks' time and I was very fortunate to have George on hand to help. In the piedmont and mountains, most shingles are rived from quality red oak. Once, in the regions, they were made from chestnut; that was before the great chestnut blight decimated this great tree. Shingles in the coastal plains were made from cypress or white cedar. Rather than to continually having to climb up the ladder with a few shingles, I rigged up two long runners, like a railroad track with a small wheeled dolly. Then with a pulley on top of the building, the man at the bottom could pull the shingles up with a rope. Once we had a supply on top, we could then start to nail the shingles. Working without haste, so as to avoid an accident, we finished the roof in three days.

When I mentioned to Betty that George and I would spend more time on the mountain, so he could point out some things that probably I wasn't aware of, Betty said, "Well, young man, you can march up that rock pile you bought and bring me back some more garnets. While I'm working my fingers to the bone, you don't need to spend your time up there just piddling around." "Yes, Mam." I answered – rather meekly. I had to assure my wife that we would bring down a bunch of garnets.

Buck and I drove to Whitesides and found George sitting on his front porch, staring off in the distance, as if in deep concentration. He motioned me to a chair; I gathered it was a greeting. Sometimes, Indians are like that, talkative at times, but silent for the most part. You more or less have to draw them out in conversation. "Yes, let's take a day or so and spend on the mountain." He answered. "Well, my wife has instructed me to bring back some more garnets; she needs those for her jewelry work." "You mentioned that you had never been on the top peak yet; I wanted to take you up there, then we can circle down to the other side and bring back garnets. If we get an early start from the Overhang camp, we can make the trek back to camp by late afternoon." George pointed out.

Taking enough food to last a couple of days, we struck out up the orchard and headed for the Overhang. George remarked that "It looked like the apple crop would be good in the fall." Since Tommy

Holden had cleared the orchard, the trees had received more sunlight and therefore, were producing more fruit.

July sun made the climb unpleasant and it was a welcomed relief when we left the orchard and entered the forest above. Moving up the white oak ridge, it was apparent that the acorn crop would be slim in the fall. White oaks only produce a full crop at intervals, of three or four years. Other species such as black oaks, red oaks or Spanish oaks, sometimes, bear seed when white oaks are not.

George foraged in front; his eyes sweeping the forest ahead; funny he never seemed to look down, and I wondered why he never stumbled or tripped over a vine. Nearing the top of the ridge, we swung to the right, crossing several shallow hollows; I noticed many large wild grape vines in these places. We reached the Overhang around noontime, but it would be too late to attempt the climb today, so most of the afternoon was spent cutting and stashing firewood.

Next morning, with an early start, we reached the trail that led up to the pass, following this a few yards, George then veered off to the right, along a faint footpath. This was a long diagonal path, which roughly paralleled the pass trail for a long ways, leading ever upward. Finally, the path reversed itself in the opposite direction and we broke out on top. I was stunned to see that a flat area of perhaps two acres behind the top was a marsh, with a small pond in its' center. Aquatic plants, such as reeds, cattails and small lily pads ringed the pond. Several small bog turtles moved slowly around, paying scant attention to us.

The pinnacle towered above the flat for another hundred feet and we scrambled to its' top. Suffice it is to say, the view from here, in all directions, projected a panoramic scene, stretching for untold miles. After we had lingered for several minutes, mesmerized at the view, George cautioned that we should be on our way, for storm clouds start forming soon. To be caught up here in a summer storm would not be safe. Warm air, rising from far below, would cool quickly, forming clouds and the fierce storms at this time of year.

Following the crest of the mountain westward, we descended to a point just above the creek, which formed the west boundary of my property. Then turning to the north and scaling down the mountain, the wire fence boundary was reached. Following this for a mile, we came to the garnet location. It was fortunate that George had sounded the alarm about the prospects for a summer storm; now high above us, thunder and lightening roared. Soon, the whole mountain would be covered by sheets of rain.

Without hesitation, we each selected a chunk of garnet bearing rock and started eastward for the path leading to the top of the pass. In a short span, the squall reached us and we were drenched to the bone in a matter of seconds. A slippery trail, combined with having to carry a heavy chunk of rock, was indescribable! By the time we reached the top of the pass, the storm had already abated, but now a blinding fog had set in. The visibility was so hampered, that we could only see for a few feet ahead, and at times, had to feel the way with our feet!

After what seemed like an eternity, the fog thinned and we reached the Overhang. Now, ringing wet and shivering cold, we were a miserable lot! George quickly shaved some fat pine, struck a match and started a fire. I kidded him for not using a stick, Indian fashion, to start a fire. "Well, matches were one good things the white man taught us." He laughed. With a roaring fire now going, we stripped off our wet clothes and hung them over a pole, close to the fire. Now, setting buck naked; I broke out a bottle of Jack Daniel, taking a strong swig, I passed the bottle to George. Shortly, our spirits began to soar!

The night was spent under less than pleasant circumstances and next morning we decided to return to Cashiers. George wanted to take Betty and I to Cherokee to meet his two nephews. Betty was surprised when we drove up, but after I explained the circumstances and that George wanted to make the trip to Cherokee, she was all for it.

Next morning, George drove up in his 1942 Buick Roadmaster. Pale green in color and in immaculate condition, it was an imposing sigh. More imposing than the car, however, was George, himself. Dressed in a dark gray suit with a blue tie and topped with a black fedora hat, he would double for any Hollywood actor! We were much perplexed, because neither of us had any dress clothes, not even any that were fit to wear to church. George assured us that to any clothes we chose to wear would be fine.

Betty and Buck road in the rear. Buck sat very stiff at first, but later relaxed and on occasion, would hang his head out the window. We turned west at Sylva and passed through Dillsboro. Cherokee was only a short distance from here.

George headed straight to the police station. Phillip and Henry

Owl were patrol officers on the Council. The reservation, comprising some twenty thousand acres, with a population of ten thousand people, had to be patrolled by a number of officers. As we entered, Henry was behind a desk and when he looked up and saw his uncle, he quickly rose to his feet and rushed over and embraced George. Both men broke out at once, speaking rapidly in the Cherokee language. We stood by amused, then Henry apologized. "Haven't seen my uncle in quite a spell. Phillip is on patrol and should be in shortly." We were led to a lounge, large enough to afford some privacy; here, Henry brought us up to date on the workings of the Council Police.

Interested in the type of crime that the police had to deal with, I asked about this. "Well, you see, most of our problems deal with alcohol related things settled within family circles. Federal crimes are settled in federal courts. At this point, Phillip walked in and Harry introduced us. Phillip was slightly larger than Henry, but both men strongly favored each other.

As the brothers were close to my age and both had served in WWII, I asked them about their military experience. "We were marine snipers, but served in different companies; you see, the Service did not allow brothers in the same company." Henry pointed out. Henry asked about my own military experience during the war and I touched briefly on mine, serving in China and other southwestern Asian countries.

The brothers had some free time, so we drove to the Oconaluftee Indian Village. Here we got a glimpse of early Cherokee life. Most interesting to Betty and me were the many crafts, such as weaving, pottery and woodworking. Later, we visited the Museum of the Cherokee Indian. So interesting and intriguing was all this, that we had spent the better of two hours without realizing how much time had passed.

Henry led us to his favorite restaurant. As several diners stared; perhaps wondering why two uniformed officers were escorting us around! The thought never occurred to me that someday these two brothers would play an important part in our future. When we finally paid out respects and went back to the car; poor Buck, he was fast asleep.

As George drove us back to Cashiers, I thought how fortunate that Betty and I were to have friends as the Owls.

CHAPTER IV

The Discoveries

"**B**ob, dear, I'll be needing more garnets in a day or two." Betty called out. "Yes, honey, I'll get busy right away." Well, I knew what that meant – hours, stooped over a chunk of rock, hammering and pecking away, extracting the small crystal, until my fingers and hands were so numb and cramped that I could hardly grip the tools. "Why oh why," had I not gone into the lumber business with Fred Barnes when he had pleaded with me to do so. Now, we could be in Wilmington, living the good life; a mild climate, fresh seafood the year round, sunny beaches and most of all, a good income! Instead, here we were, working our fingers to the bone, trying to make enough money to pay our taxes and expenses, without having to dip into dwindling savings. Pangs of remorse, guilt swept through my mind, feeling more pain for my wife than myself. "Oh well, Butler, you dug your fox hole, now live in it," I cursed under my breath.

Going to the shelf, I picked up the smallest chunk of garnet laden rock and took it out back; seating comfortably in the shade, the laborious work began. Buck with head resting on front feet, was snoring away. "Buck, you old rascal, how lucky you are, nothing to do but eat, sleep and fart."

Extracting tiny garnets is frustrating work. First, visible crystals around the surface of the chunk are chipped out, then the rock must be split in half as more are exposed. The two halves of the rock are again halved, and so on down until all the garnets are exposed.

Rays from the afternoon sun were more slanting now when the last crystal was extracted. My! How my fingers ached! Standing up and straightening my stiff back, I had to pause a few minutes before I could walk. Taking a coffee can full of tiny stones in to Betty, "Here honey, hope these will do you till tourist season ends."

Suddenly remembering the chunk of rock that held the protruding knife handle crystal, I took it outside and began chipping around it. It was probably two inches in diameter and already jutted out a couple of inches. Shortly, it came free and I anticipated making a beautiful knife handle from it. That is of course, if I could catch Betty in a good mood, so she could slice the thin pieces on her diamond saw! The piece, with mingling white quartz and faded emeralds would be really attractive, I reasoned.

Tired and numb with the day's work, I slipped the extrusion in a pocket and stopped to pick up the chunk of rock, thinking of examining it later for more knife material. As I lifted the rock to the fading sunlight, a tiny glint of bright green reflected in my eyes. Curious, I spotted a pea sized green object in the rock's depression, from where the knife piece was extracted.

"Well, I've got to see what this is I whispered. Once again, I picked up my pick and small hammer in partially numb fingers and began chipping around and around the object as it got larger. Taking care not to make a miss lick, in a few minutes, I knew what it was – a six sided, brilliant green, an emerald! All at once, I forgot about my numb fingers, as I worked furiously around the piece and shortly, I held it up – what a sight! "Bob, supper will be ready in a few minutes, better come in and get ready." Betty called. "Yes, I'll be there, give me a few more minutes." I hollered back.

Wondering if there might be more of these beautiful things within the chunk of rock, I took up the larger mason's hammer and split the rock in half. There! Lay another gem, partially embedded along the long axis of the rock. This one was easy to pick out. Shaking with excitement, I threw down the tool and strode into the store.

Betty was already seated at the table and had begun to eat; walking straight to the kitchen cabinet, I pulled down a bottle of Jack Daniel and poured both of us half a glass of the golden brown liquid. Shoving a glass towards my wife, I demanded. "drink this." She eyed me suspiciously, but lifted the glass and began to sip; I did likewise. "Something is wrong." Betty said, "You're acting strangely." Wanting to have some fun, I kidded, "How much did you make fooling with those garnets, today?" "Why, I made five bracelets, that's probably a hundred dollars; now smarty, how much did you make?" Betty's temper was rising. "If you really want to know, I honestly couldn't say, but if you multiply two thousand karats by $50, then, that could possibly be a hundred thousand dollars. Of course, all this depends upon the quality of what I'm talking about." "On the quality of what?" Betty exploded "These." I responded, shoving the two huge crystals in her hand.

Betty, in a state of shock, while she looked at the gems, her eyes widening by the second, gasped. "Where did you get these?" "They came from that "rock pile of a mountain" you've been ribbing me about." I brought down a chunk of rock to get a knife handle made from a pretty stone in it and placed it on the shelf a few months ago. "You mean that thing was lying up there gathering dust all this time and you didn't know what was inside it; that's incredible! What are we going to do?"

"Honey, I've got to get back up there and see if there are more of these; there are tons of rock just like the rock that it came from lying around. Best thing to do, is camp out at the Overhang and I can cross the mountain and work during the day. You and Buck can stay at the Overhang and fix the meals, I figure, I can work three or four hours a day and get back to camp before dark. This is much easier than having to carry a chunk of rock all the way back to Cashiers!" "George can bring up supplies from the Norton place." "Well, are you going to tell him what you found?" "No honey, later I'll have to, but not now." "For the time being, I'll just tell him that we want to camp up there and I might get some more garnets, in the meantime. "Now, let's get ready and leave tomorrow."

Both of us spent a fitful night, tossing and turning, probably brought on by the discovery and what the future might bring on.

Reaching the Norton place by ten o'clock, we found George busy working on the building; he was surprised to learn that we were going to camp on the mountain. "Yes, I'll be glad to keep you supplied with food and whatever you need." Good old George! We would leave for the mountain in the morning.

That evening, Betty prepared a good stew and for dessert, blackberry pie. I'm sure it must have been a welcome relief for George, with his style of cooking! After supper, we sat out on the porch, having a drink of my favorite, JD. Usually George was quiet, and it took about his second drink to get him started on what we wanted to hear – tales about his past and about legends of his people.

"What about rattlesnakes? George, are there many up there?" I wanted to know. "Rattlesnakes? Yes, there are plenty up there and some are large." "Let me tell you what happened a year ago, you won't believe it. I was camping in late summer and the night was pitch black. Had built up a good fire after supper. You know, after I lost my only son in WWII and my wife a year ago, I was pretty depressed, so camping up there seemed to help. But anyway, I took out my fiddle and began to play and after a few minutes of playing, I noticed a movement in the dim firelight a few yards away. Looking closer, I saw a huge triangular head starring at me and weaving back and forth. It must have been the music that had attracted him to the place. Anyway, to say the least, I was shocked and scared, almost out of my wits. My gun was twenty feet away, lint up against the wall and all I could do was to keep playing and praying. You know that monster just kept swaying back and forth, seemingly keeping time with the music. I began to play softer and softer, and finally, that snake just lowered to the ground and disappeared in the dark! As far as I know, he may still be around because I get a whiff of snake every time I camp up there." "Why George, that's amazing." Betty and I exclaimed. George continued, "You know, we Cherokee, hold rattlesnakes in reverence, we don't harm them, they don't seem to pay much attention to us; we just give them plenty of space when they're encountered."

Starting after a "lumberman's" breakfast next morning, we headed for the Overhang. With two canvas cots, sleeping bags and all the food that three of us could carry, the going was slow and we rested often. I also carried my small tools, since a large rock hammer had already been left at the emerald site. July's sun bore down, but shortly as we climbed, the temperature began to drop, and by ten o'clock we reached the Overhang.

George rested a few minutes with us, then returned to the Norton place. He promised to check on us in two days. He cautioned us to be careful in the Pass, as we came near the large boulders. "It's a snake hangout so by pass it."

It was too late now for me to go on over and do some work; I wouldn't be able to make it back to camp before dark. We spent the rest of the day gathering wood and getting the camp in order.

I sternly warned Buck to stay in camp and not wander around, knowing full well the minute I turned my back, he would nose around somewhere. The day had been full for us, so we turned in early.

At the crack of the day, I roused Betty and while I brewed coffee, she fixed breakfast. Soon, after eating, I was off to the other side. Traveling up the great pass, I remembered George's advise and skirted the large boulders. On the way up, grouse after grouse, flushed in front of me. Sunlight crept slowly down the mountain side in the pass and finally I broke out on top. Resting a few minutes, I started down.

As the emerald location was above the old fence boundary, I turned at what I thought was the elevation of the work place. The going was steep and rough. "A road could never be built along this route without great expense." I thought. Reaching the work place, I glanced at my watch. It was nine thirty; it had only taken me an hour and half to get here.

Pausing a few minutes, I took up the large rock hammer and broke off a chunk of calcite rock, which was convenient to chisel on. Sure enough, after a few hammer blows an emerald reflected in the sunlight. Using a small hammer and chisel, the crystal was extracted in a short while. The crystal, not very large, appeared to be of the same quality as those I had extracted at Cashiers. Splitting the chunk of rock in half, another crystal was exposed. Within thirty minutes, I had uncovered two nice gems. For the next three hours I worked. So engrossed in the effort that the departure time almost slipped up on me, now, it was time to head toward camp. So busy with the work, that I had lost count of the crystals, and was surprised to find fourteen in the pile. Not bad for four hours of work. Distant thunder in the mountains toward the west warned that trouble might lie ahead!

Wrapping the emeralds tightly in a cloth, so they would not grate against each other, I placed the tools under a small ledge and lost no time toward camp.

The way back towards the trail was rough; at least, I had two free hands to steady me, if I should lose my footing. At last, the trail! Now the going towards the top was better, although very steep. The rumble in the west was increasing and I hurried down the Pass, praying that it wouldn't catch me. We failed to bring a change of clothes, so if I got drenched, it would mean stripping off and drying my clothes by the fire. Coming close to the large boulders, I skirted them, losing a minute. As the boulders were only twenty minutes from camp, I knew I could beat the storm, for it was still further west. Entering the Overhang, I was welcomed with hugs and barks.

"I know that you must be exhausted," Betty said, "and here is just the medicine for you", as she handed me a glass of sour mash. She patiently waited for my day's account of things. The drink had it's effect and I bragged about the fourteen gems. Buck laid his head against my knee; it felt warm and I stroked his shaggy mane. "He hasn't been a good boy today." Betty said. "He was out there, scratching at that ground hog hole and I had to go get him." "You bad boy, you'll never learn." I scolded, gently.

The storm finally came, roaring in, lightening struck far above around the peak, but the thunder was frightening. Buck and Betty cringed close to me; at least we were dry and well protected.

Since the Overhang faced southeast and most bad weather came from the northwest, the Overhang protected it's visitors. "I will have to go back over tomorrow." I said. "Fred will need enough crystals to show three or four companies." "I wish I could go with you, can't I?" Betty pleaded. "No, honey, it would slow me down and if a storm caught us it would be dangerous."

The storm hadn't lasted but a few minutes, however, it left a chilly, damp night. We built a roaring fire to keep us cozy. Good dry wood was an absolute necessity to have stored under the Overhang. We slept very well; knowing that my day's work had paid off!

The next day was a repeat of yesterday, although I only was able to extract eleven gems. By the time I had gotten back to camp, my legs were like rubber. Walking up and down a mountain takes three times as much effort as doing so on gentle ground.

We decided that twenty-five crystals and the two that I had extracted in Cashiers, would suffice for Fred. When we reached the Norton house, George was in the act of coming up with more supplies. He had been concerned about the storm and asked about it.

Stopping by Mike's Service Station, I placed a call to Fred. Fortunately, he was in the office. "Bob, great to hear from you; how are things?" "Things are fine, could I perhaps come down tomorrow and look at the flooring for the Norton place?" "Why sure, bring Betty and stay a few days." "Thanks, but maybe next time, I want to look at the lumber and have it brought up, George needs it." I tried to conceal the urgency in my voice. "well, I'll expect you tomorrow then." Fred said.

Leaving early next morning, I stopped in Charlotte around noon, eating a light lunch; then topping off the gas tank. After being used to the cool mountains, the lower piedmont and coastal plains certainly were a change. The heat and humidity really got to me!

I rolled into Wilmington at three. Fred had been expecting me and took me into the office. He asked about Betty and how things were "up there in the mountains". I inquired about Rachel and about how things were going with the mill.

After exchanging pleasantries, news and recent events, I suddenly asked if we could have complete privacy. "Why sure Bob." Fred looked somewhat surprised. "I hope nothing is wrong." "No Fred, everything is fine. I need your complete confidence in something though." "The real reason I'm here could be very important to both of us." "Bob, I hope it's legal, but if it isn't, don't tell me." Good old Fred, always a straight shooter. "It's all legal, Fred, but the source and the owner, me, must be kept confidential." "O.K., then, shoot." Fred agreed.

I unrolled the crystals and spread them on the desk. At first, Fred appeared in deep shock, as he stared, wide eyed at the gems. "Where in hell did you get these things?" He gasped. "Dug them off my mountain, Fred, that rock of a mountain, that Betty ribbed me about buying." "My God! Man, they must be worth a fortune." Fred uttered, in a trembling voice. "Well, that's why I brought them to you to find out what they are worth. I know that you mentioned several times, that you bought jewelry for Rachel while you were in New York. Now, do you think that you could take these up there to several jewelers and try to see what they're worth and maybe sell them?"

Fred was silent a few moments, as he fingered one of the largest emeralds. "I was thinking, yes, sure, for several years I have bought expensive jewelry from and old Jewish company, Finklestein and Finklestein. They are one of the largest firms in New York, both wholesale and retail. They also manufacture all types of jewelry. Yes, I'll take them up there." "In that case Fred, if you can get a fair price and sell them, I'll give you ten percent of whatever they bring." Fred wanted to know what the prospects for more crystals were and I told him that I thought they were unlimited. Naturally, he was elated. "Fred, until I can develop the mine, with all it's security, this must be kept secret; not even Rachel should know." "I understand" Fred agreed.

"Now, let's close up shop and go home, we will go to Faircloths tonight and eat seafood! After locking the crystal in a huge iron safe, we left for Fred's on Oleander Drive, east. Rachel greeted me warmly as usual. She had just been puttering in the back in a huge flower garden. Even at home, she was always well dressed and the only time she wasn't wearing exquisite jewelry was when she didn't work outside. Had she shed her work gloves and put on jewelry, she would be ready to meet the public! Was a good thing that Fred was a successful business man to keep her dressed in that manner, I thought.

At Faircloths that evening, Fred was quieter than usual; I knew why of course; the responsibility and it's implications, that I had suddenly thrust upon him, had to be the reason! Fred broke his silence by telling Rachel that he must go to New York in a day or two to settle a lumber account. The fresh seafood platter, huge and delicious, was almost more than I could handle, and I longed to have Betty with me to enjoy one like it. Fred promised to have the flooring lumber delivered in a couple of days.

Early the next morning, I left for Cashiers, confident that Fred would do his best to find out the value of the emeralds and possibly sell them.. I told Fred, upon leaving that if the emeralds panned out to be what we both hoped for, he might be working for me someday. "Bob, you're right, the lumber business, being what it's probably coming to, I may be working for you."

After checking with the mill foreman and seeing what else was taking place, Fred drove back in town and went to his special shoe shop. He was always having field boots repaired. Having to do his own timber cruising for the mill, took a heavy toll on leather. He had decided to have half moon pockets sewn inside of the back of engineer boots; this he figured would accommodate the 27 jewels safely. It would be somewhat uncomfortable, but at least, safe. The shoe shop assured him that they would be ready that afternoon.

Later that afternoon, Fred placed a call to Finklestein and Finklestein in New York, advising them that he was coming up the next day. They looked forward to his visit, anticipating of course a profitable jewelry sale for Rachel. They were somewhat puzzled because he did not mention that his wife would not accompany him, however. They offered to made reservations at the Waldorf-Astoria for him and he thanked them.

Wilmington was in the process of expanding it's airport to accommodate Piedmont Airlines. This would be ready by spring; for now, Fred would have to go up by rail; the Atlantic Coastline RR. The next morning, he left at seven, expecting to be there by one o'clock. This train was a special and there would be few stops along the way.

Settling in comfortably, he watched the scenery flash by; gradually the expanse of pine forest gave way to more open farmland as Rocky Mount, North Carolina, neared. Fred felt a pang of remorse, for how long would the beautiful pine forest last, until everything might change into small open farmlands? After all, the forests were his livelihood! It was nearing the last of July and the fields of corn, now turning brown, would be ready to harvest in a couple of months. From Richmond on, the farms became smaller and only small patches of timber remained.

On schedule, the train pulled into Grand Central at one o'clock. Fred had carried only a medium size leather suitcase, which he hadn't checked, and he was off the train at once. Hailing a cab, he went directly to the hotel and checked in. The appointment was at two, which gave him time to check in and grab a quick lunch.

Finklestein and Finklestein in a large brownstone, was located in the heart of the main shopping district on 5th Avenue. Jewelry stores, exclusive clothing and haberdashery stores, and furniture stores were everywhere. As Fred walked in, he didn't have to be announced, for Joseph, the eldest brother was waiting for him. Both men had built up a warm relationship over the past few years. Joseph called for Aaron, the younger brother, and then informed his secretary that they did not wish to be disturbed.

Seating comfortably, the men exchanged pleasant formalities as Aaron walked in and shook hands. Then, Joseph said, "Fred, I assume that this is not exactly a buying trip?" "Your assumption is correct. Now what I am going to show you is lawful, but must be kept in the strictest confidence, as far as the source and ownership is concerned." "I understand." Joseph nodded.

Reaching into his engineer's boots, Fred spread the 27 crystals on the huge mahogany desk in front of the brothers. Joseph and Aaron stared bug-eyed and speechless for long seconds. "My God, you've been walking around with those things in your boots, here in New York City, incredible!:" Joseph exclaimed. "Well, it was the only way under the present that I could think of." Fred answered. "Joseph, I brought these things to you, hoping that you would place a value on them, and perhaps find me a buyer." Joseph thought a few seconds, then "I can do that Fred, but you realize it will take some time." "Perhaps tomorrow late, I can give you an answer." "That would be appreciated very much, Joseph; but let me leave most of the crystals with you and take three or four elsewhere; the owner requested me to get several different evaluations." "I understand but, you must be very careful up here." Joseph cautioned. Fred left nineteen crystals and took eight with him. As he was leaving, Joseph asked Fred if he would like to have dinner with them this evening. "Thank you Joseph, but I didn't bring any dress clothes this trip. That isn't important, Fred, how about six, we'll pick you up. "This will be fine, Joseph."

Fred proceeded up Fifth Avenue and stopped in front of a large jewelry store, Rubin and Son, Jewelry, Wholesale and Retail. This was a large place and Fred entered. He was immediately approached by a smiling clerk, anxious no doubt to make a quick sale to this roughly dressed man, whom he probably took for a rich Texas oil man. "May I help you?" The clerk asked. "Yes, you may, I want to speak to the owner, or your general manager, preferably the owner." "Very well, sir, just a minute." A minute later, Fred was ushered into an expansive office. A fat, bald man, seemingly too large to stand, remained seated. "Yes?" He said abruptly. "Well, sir, I thought you might be able to place a value on these." Fred answered, producing two of the stones.

The man's eyes widened, as he turned one of the crystals, this way and that, in pudgy fingers. At once, he pressed a button and a young man appeared. "See what you think of this", he handed one of the emeralds to the man. Holding the stone up to the light, he finally uttered, "well Mr. Rubin, it looks good, but I'd have to study it in the lab before I could be sure of it's quality." Now Rubin seemed more friendly. "If you leave these with us, I can give you a more definitive answer by tomorrow noon." "Very well sir, give me a receipt for the two and I will be back by noon, tomorrow."

Fred proceeded down Fifth Avenue and stopped by a brownstone building. "Romero Incorporated" the huge gold sign read. The large glass front displayed all kinds of jewelry, from watches to golden crucifixes, to figures of religious nature. It was probably non Jewish; perhaps Italian, Fred reasoned. As he walked in, the place reminded Fred of a giant pawnshop. Several clerks stood around; a large olive-complexioned man was behind the counter. "I would like to speak to the manager." Fred said. "You're speaking to him." The man behind the counter answered. Well, I take it that you buy and sell jewelry, would you put a value on these and make me an offer?" The man motioned to a man far across the room and a small stooped shouldered man, wearing a shaded cap appeared. "See what you think of these." The manager said. The small man lifted one of the crystals to the light and studied it a few minutes. "I'll have to examine it in my lab, it'll take a few minutes." While Fred was waiting the results, the manager asked him where he was from, since it was obvious that he wasn't a New Yorker. "Why, I'm from Louisiana, right across from the Texas border." "How did you come by these?" The manager queried. "I was over in Texas, near the Mexican border and bought them from a Mexican; I figured they must have come from Columbia, through Central America.

Presently, the technician came over and whispered to the manager. "The technician says they are of poor quality, but I will give you five hundred dollars apiece for them, that's in cash." Trying to sound interested in the deal, Fred answered that he would have to consult with his wife, first and if she would agree, he'd come back in the morning. He took the two crystals and left, knowing that he had probably made a mistake.

As soon as Fred departed, the manager called one of his clerks over. "It's obvious that the man was lying. "Hell, I've been to Louisiana many times, he don't talk like them Frenches down there." "Put a tail on him and report back to me."

Promptly at six o'clock, the Finklesteins came by the hotel for Fred. Their chauffeur drove them Club 21, one of the most exclusive dining clubs in New York. The floor was marble, with carpeted isles. A six piece band played all the while. Mahogany tables, linen covered, with sterling silverware, bespoke of a setting for the elite, only.

Throughout the evening, Fred was anxious to know what Aaron was finding out about the crystals, however Aaron was non-committal. Mostly, the conversation hinged around the business.

65

After leaving Romero's earlier in the afternoon, the tail followed Fred to the hotel. As soon as Fred picked up his key and gone to his room, the tail bribed the clerk with a twenty dollar bill. "he's registered under the name of Fred Barnes, from Wilmington, North Carolina, the clerk informed. "He has stayed here many times, before." "Well, keep me informed, it will be worth your time." The tail said, slipping the clerk another twenty. "Here's my phone number." "Thank you very much sir." The delighted clerk beamed. "I sure will."

Finally back at Club 21, the conversation swung around to the jewelry business. "If your stones prove of real value, what are the chances of getting a steady supply?" Joseph wanted to know. "Although, this is too early to assure you, my guess is that the possibility would be very good. The owners and of course I can't reveal their identity, probably want to open a public mine." Fred reasoned that since Joseph had approached the subject, this might be a clue to what Aaron was finding. Well, he would just have to be patient until the morrow.

At two o'clock next day, Fred went straight to Rubin and Son. This time Rubin was extremely friendly and greeted Fred warmly. "Come on in the office, my friend." Jovially he patted Fred on the back and led him into the office. "Mr. Barnes", Rubin began, "your stones are very nice, the two totaled 1100 karats and at $50 dollars a karat, we can offer you$55,000 dollars." Fred pondered a few minutes, after all didn't Bob want three estimates, at least? He decided to take the offer. "It will take about twenty minutes to transfer the money and receive confirmation." Rubin said. "Now, I would like to buy more crystals, perhaps on a steady basis, what are the prospects?" "Mr. Rubin, I can't assure you at this point without consulting with the owners, but your offer on these seems fair and I will keep in touch with you." In a few minutes, the transaction was confirmed. They shook hands and Fred left for Finklesteins.

Aaron had only processed half of the stones when Fred arrived; Joseph apologized profusely, assuring the others would be finished by ten o'clock next day. Then, Joseph asked if Fred had obtained satisfaction from the other two people. "Yes, from Rubin and Son. I thought the transaction was fair, especially when I told him that I had talked to you." Joseph smiled at that. "At Romero's, I didn't think the offer was in line so I declined their offer." Joseph probably wanted to know their offer and also what Rubin's offer was, but he kept silent.

By ten thirty next morning, the balance of the stones had been completed and Joseph presented the results. "The 19 stones totaled 9500 karats and at $50 dollars a karat, we can offer you $475,000." "Well, I have the two that I didn't sell to Romero's, do you want them?" "Take a look at them Aaron and see if they're the same as these and weigh them." Aaron left and was back in a few minutes. "They are the same. They total 900 karats." "Alright." Joseph said. "That's $45,000 dollars." Fred agreed and Joseph totaled the sum, $520,000 dollars. "Then transfer the sum to First Merchants in Wilmington. In less than fifteen minutes, the confirmation came through. The men shook hands and Fred assured them that he would be in touch. Fred kept the remaining six.

The jeweler at Romero's was faced with a dilemma, for after all, he was not the first to be contacted by this southern ignoramus, who was foolish enough to be carrying around a fortune in his pocket? He could have this man followed, find out his source of emeralds and perhaps fall into a fortune. Did he ,however, have the resources to capitalize on the situation? If he plunged ahead and bungled the undertaking, and the big boss, Director, found out about it, then he might very well wind up in the bottom of the Hudson River, encased in a cement suitcase. Director was head of the New York Mafia, North Eastern Group. Fortunately, the Jeweler made a wise decision, for himself; he placed a call to his boss.

"Director, this is Jeweler, there is something important that I think you should be made aware of." "Jeweler, and that is?" Director said. "Well, sir, yesterday this southerner, named Fred Barnes from Wilmington, North Carolina, came into my store with two beautiful emeralds that he claimed he got while in Texas. He was carrying these around in his pocket and wanted me to put a value and price on them; can you imagine such stupidity?" :Get to the point, Jeweler." Director rasped. "The point is sir, that I think the man was lying because I had him followed to his hotel and my man bribed the clerk there for information. I offered him $500 cash, apiece for the stones, but he declined. He obviously knew what they were. Also, my tail followed him to Finklestein." "You did well, Jeweler, now, if Barnes goes back to Wilmington, I want him followed. I'll put Lieutenant on him, my best man. Keep me informed at once." "Who is your man tailing Barnes?" "Sir, he is Mario Stansi and he's camping out at the hotel." "Very well Jeweler, but one thing, be careful around Finklestein, they are supporters of the Massad; we don't want to cross them sons of bitches." "Have Stansi keep in touch with Lieutenant and I'll handle this from now on; you keep in touch with me." "Thank you, Director." Jeweler said, hoping that he had scored a few points.

The Director picked up his telephone and dialed a number. "Lieutenant? This is Director, I want you to keep in touch with one of my tails; his name is Mario Stansi and he is camping out at the Waldorf-Astoria. When he gives you the word, I want you to follow a man by the name of Fred Barnes, when he goes back to Wilmington, North Carolina. Barnes flashed some valuable emeralds to one of my contacts; I want to know the source of those crystals." "I'll leave at once." Lieutenant said, hoping this would be an exciting new adventure.

After leaving Finklestein's Fred was so elated over his good luck with the two transactions he could hardly wait to get back to Wilmington and inform the Butlers of the good news. It was approaching five o'clock and his train would leave at six. Checking out of the hotel, he caught a cab and rushed to the RR Station. Lieutenant was just seconds behind him. Fred would arrive in Wilmington around one o'clock.

On Fred's instruction, I called Rachel at eight o'clock and was surprised that Fred answered. "Bob, you and Betty come at once, the "timber business" is looking up, can you be here this afternoon?" "Yes, we can come Fred, but I don't have time to go leave Buck with George at the Norton place; can we bring him?" "Yes, bring Buck, we'll see you this afternoon."

Fred turned to Rachel, "The Butler's are coming today; Bob is going to help me decide on an important tract of timber." "Well Fred, isn't this rather sudden?" Rachel looked puzzled. "It is honey, but it's important to us." "Very well, perhaps Betty and I can shop and do some things while you take care of business."

We hastily got some clothes together and were on our way by ten o'clock; the trip would put us in Wilmington by five o'clock, depending of course on how many stops we made. One thing is certain, when you're traveling with a woman and a dog, forget about keeping to a certain schedule! It was approaching towards the last of July and as we left the coolness of Jackson County and descended toward South Carolina, the heat really hit us. Poor Buck, at least he could seek some relief , sticking his shaggy head out the window. At least I, on the drivers' side could get some relief, if one could call blasting hot air relief! Betty would suffer the most.

As we went through Greenville, South Carolina, Betty reminded me of the good times she had while going to Furman University there. "Well, at least it must have been a little cooler here than my hotter than hell days in Athens, Georgia, I reminded her. "I suffered just as much in Georgia as you; you drug me down there when we got married – remember?" You just can't get ahead of a woman; at least not me!

The region from Greenville through Spartanburg and then on through Gaffney, is red clay country. Also, it's probably the best peach country in the US. I have never tasted a peach, grown elsewhere, that has the flavor that is grown here.

Charlotte, the hub of North Carolina industry, is perhaps the fastest growing section in North Carolina. We stopped here for lunch, while Buck crawled under the car for shade. He was rewarded with a big hamburger afterwards. Wilmington was two hours away.

Ah, 1307 Oleander Drive, what a relief at last. Fred and Rachel came out to greet us and as soon as the excitement was over, Fred carried our scant bags inside. Rachel led the way to an air conditioned den, as a middle aged Negro maid served us ice cold lemonade. The conversation hinged around our activities in Cashiers and they asked about George. "Couldn't get along without him; he's working on the floor now, boy, you should listen to some of the tales he spins." I laughed. Rachel asked Betty about the jewelry business, "isn't it excruciating work, dear?" "Yes, excruciating, but rewarding, knowing that the things you make are worn by lots of people," Betty said.

I could sense that Fred was eager to get me aside, so he could talk, so I brought up the subject of timber. Fred suggested that he and I retire to the rear, large screened porch. A huge ceiling fan, rotating overhead, kept the porch very comfortable. Nearby, large magnolia trees also helped to modify the temperature. Beyond the trees was Rachel's beloved flower garden.

No sooner than we were seated, Fred began. "Bob, it was a fortune. I made two sales, totaling $520,000. Rubin and Son, $45,000 and Finklestein and Finklestein, $475,000. That is fantastic, Fred, and I want you to take out your ten percent commission. This is deposited in The First Merchants Bank here. Tomorrow, I will take you and Betty to the bank so the account can be transferred into your name. Later you and I can go out to the mill and talk at length."

Rachel realized that Betty and I were tired after the long drive. She had prepared a light dinner, afterward, we talked for a while, making plans for the morrow. We retired early.

Early the next morning, just before sunrise, Lieutenant stopped in front of 1307 Oleander Drive and lifting binoculars, read the license plate on the Butler Ford. From the plate number he could determine the owner and location from the North Carolina Department of Motor Vehicles.

At breakfast, Fred announced that Betty and I should go with him to the bank. "they want to set up an account to use when in Wilmington," he nodded to Rachel.

First and Merchants, located at the intersection of lower Market and third Streets is an old brick building, dating back to the turn of the century. Outward looks did not belie what the bank represented inside, however. Without doubt, it probably processed a third of financial business for a hundred miles around. One had to arrive early in the morning, otherwise, the unfortunate customer spent a few harrowing minutes finding a parking space!

The transaction inside took about twenty minutes. After Fred's commission of $52,000, I took out $5,000 cash. Betty and I had on deposit there, $463,000. From the $5,000, I gave Betty a thousand dollars to shop for the day. As we left the bank, we were unaware that someone had snapped our pictures.

It was Saturday and since the mill was closed, we took Buck to the mill with us; there he could roam around the log yard and get some exercise. I could also keep an eye on the rascal! The women could shop and later we would all go out to Wrightsville Beach for the weekend.

We sat on a slick barked, young cypress log; the temperature had not risen much yet, so it was good to be outside. I took out my old Case pocket knife and began to slice on the log. It seems I can always do my best thinking when relaxed with a pocket knife!

We discussed at length plans for developing the emeralds. First and for a long time, I told Fred, we must keep the location a secret. Only when I am ready to announce the opening of the mine, can we reveal it's source. "Bob, you've just got to have a telephone installed." Fred urged. "We will be constantly calling each other from now on." I agreed to that. "Another thing, to throw people off the track, let's substitute lumber and timber for emeralds, when on the phone." "Good idea, Fred." I agreed. "another thing Bob, the Rubins' and Finklesteins' want to know when they can receive more stones." "That will be my first priority when I get back to Cashiers, Fred." Another urgent matter that had been on my mind was to try and buy the large mountain tract of land that joined my property. Another thing that came to mind was that if the emerald business really took off, Fred might be working for me full time. "Well, Bob, the lumber business, with it's competition, I may wind up working for you." Fred agreed.

It was getting towards lunch time and Fred suggested that we go home and get some lunch, then, head for Wrightsville Beach. The girls had already come in from their shopping spree and Betty had to tell me of all the clothes she had bought. After all, it had been almost two years since the poor girl had bought any new clothes. It made me feel so good to see her in such an upbeat mood! After lunch, we packed our clothes and other necessities and left for Wrightsville.

Without doubt, Wrightsville Beach is by far, the nicest beach around Wilmington. It's houses facing the ocean front, were probably built at the turn of the century, or maybe even earlier. At the time of construction, they were made from original long leaf pine timber. Kept painted, the houses will probably last until a major hurricane destroys them. Numerous hurricanes have swamped Wilmington and Wrightsville in the past, but the houses still stand.

Fred's house fronted on the beach, with a large screened front porch, one could sit there, relaxed and watch all manner of humanity at play. Funny thing I've observed over the years, people , when playing in the sand or just relaxing in the water, seem to gain their second childhood. Observe that next time you're back at the beach; it's fun to watch.

The beach front is very wide at Wrightsville, even at high tide. AT Fred's, we could just walk down the steps and be in the water, in less than a minute.

Usually, when in Wilmington, the Barnes would take us to Fairclothes, a famous seafood restaurant. This time however, they took us to a new restaurant near the entrance to Wrightsville. I did not have to feel guilty this time, as I enjoyed watching my wife tackling a huge seafood platter!

Sunday was the repeat of Saturday, we went in the water, sat on the porch, or laid in the sand. Perhaps someday, we might return to Wilmington to live and enjoy it's treasures!

Monday, we bid the Barnes good bye, thanking them for their wonderful hospitality. The trip back to Cashiers was long and tiresome; we got in around six o'clock.

Tuesday morning, I asked Betty to go to Mike's Service Station and call the phone company in Sylva, asking them to install a telephone in the store, as quickly as possible. I needed to talk to George about the large tract adjoining mine on the mountain; he had mentioned it to me on several occasions in the past. I found George working on installing the floor. "The land belongs to the Rosman Flooring Company, the owner is Galloway; I've more or less looked after it for a long time." "Well, how bout we drive down there tomorrow and see if they still want to sell it?" "Yes, it suits me; they run the plant all the time; Galloway is always there." "We'll drop by the store in the morning and we'll go to Rosman."

Betty said the phone company would be over in a week; that they were busy and had lots of people waiting telephones installed.

George was at the store by eight the next morning and we left immediately for Rosman. The drive took only an hour. When we arrived, the mill was in full production. Galloway was on the telephone and talked for ten minutes, all the time eyeing us. These lumber people are certainly a tough bunch. I guess they need to be, with all the stuff around a mill, they have to contend with.

At last, he was free and George introduced me. "Yes, the land is for sale, at the right price of course." "Well, I understand it's been on the market for years, what is the price you're asking for it?" "We want twenty dollars an acre for the land, otherwise, it stays on the market." "I was prepared to make a firm offer of ten dollars and acre; that's a good price for cutover land, on steep mountain side." I pointed out. "At that price, I couldn't do that." He growled. "You know, the land has hundreds of acres of young, growing white pine on it and white pine grows like crazy." "Where do you live, are you one of them northerners, come down here to speculate on land from we poor southerners?" "No, Mr. Galloway, I'm just s poor southerner, like yourself." "Well, give me your telephone number if you got some white oak to sell." I gave Mr. Galloway Mike's Service Station number. Thanking him for his time, we left.

On the way back to Cashiers, George said, "he wants to sell, I bet you, he'll get back to you in a few days." "George, Betty and I want to spend several days at the Overhang; she has never really seen the upper part of the place. Since you are working on the Norton addition, would you mind bringing up some food for us occasionally?" "Sure, just let ,me know when to come up." "George, there is another thing that I have to bring up; it's most important to me and will probably be to you, perhaps even to your two nephews. This thing must be kept an absolute secret, at least until later." "Bob, if it's legal tell me, if it's not, keep it to yourself." "It's legal, George." "You know that green charm that you have, that's been handed down to you? Well, I have discovered probably it's source on the mountain." George was silent for several moments, I gathered, in shock. "Bob, that's amazing. I thought I knew every inch of that mountain; I can't imagine where you found it up there." "Well, George, it's on the other side, in a place so remote and rough, that no one would have any reason to be near the spot. The place wouldn't attract a hunter, or a hiker. Suffice it to say, these are emeralds and I have sold some and plan to develop a small mining operation there." "Naturally, I want you to be a part of the operation." "Well, thank you, Bob, I appreciate your confiding in me and I will keep this to myself. You remember, according to what my people told me, the charm came from a cave up there; you didn't find your things in a cave, but, I can't help believe that maybe my ancestors are right; at least, I have that feeling."

Naturally, I was disappointed for not making the deal with Galloway. The large tract would have been a buffer to my land, offering additional protection to the emerald location. I recalled what George said on the way back, yesterday. "He wants to sell, I predict that he'll call you in a few days."

The emerald location needed to be explored further; I needed to find out what it's potentials were, before spending lot's of money on it. Fred was anxious for more crystals and we certainly needed a lot of money to develop the mine, if it came to that.

Betty was as anxious as myself to go ahead and explore the situation, so she was glad when I told her that we had to spend several days at the Overhang, while I went across the mountain and worked. If she could remain at the Overhang and have me a good meal when I came in from work, maybe the strain wouldn't be so hard. After all, think of

73

walking as fast as you can, up and down a rugged mountain and then performing hard work, breaking rocks, then, having to rush back to camp before dark. Under the best of circumstances, the strain would tell on me.

We gathered food and supplies and drove to the Norton place; George was busy on the flooring. It was late in the morning when we reached the Overhang. Too late for me to even think about going across the mountain; we busied ourselves with getting the camp in order. Wood was, without doubt, one of the most important things at camp; it was always cold at night. I got busy cutting dry wood, while Betty carried it to the Overhang.

"Well, he's at it again," I raged, "that damn dog is out there at that groundhog hole. Every time I turn my back, he's out there." Afraid that Buck might get snake bitten, I rushed toward the barking. There he was growling, digging, making a nuisance of himself.

Scolding, I grabbed Buck by the collar and yanked him away from the hole. The hole itself, was perhaps two feet high, by a foot and half wide; well camouflaged by stunted growth, it would not have been detected very easily. Only an animal, sniffing around would have paid attention to it. As I pulled Buck away, I turned half away around towards the face of the mountain. For a second, an image of a giant picture frame flashed before my eyes. The frame , outlined by stunted growth, jutted out from the general face of the bare faced mountain. "That's odd." I thought. Then it struck me all at once, like a body punch. A huge slab or plate or rock some fifty feet wide, had simply separated from the mountain above, slid down and covered most of the hole.

If there was a once a cave here, then it could have been covered by this slab! Excited, I rushed back to the Overhang for the axe. Finding a long keen spruce sapling, I cut and trimmed it. Shoving the long timber into the hole, I felt no resistance, while even trying to move the pole from side to side. It was obvious now, that the hole extended much further than the length of the pole!

What to do? Yes!, the long, wild grape vines below the Overhang. I ran back to the Overhang and told Betty what had happened. "How can I pull an eighty foot grape vine down? It would take a bulldozer." "You dumb ox, take your .22 pistol and shoot the thing in two."

Betty laughed, "My God! You're smart; that's why I married you." I bragged.

The vines grew some few yards down from camp, in a rich, shallow hollow. Selecting the longest and straightest one around, I rested the little pistol against a tree and took aim. Bark flew. Bam! Again. With the third shot, the vine broke loose, almost hitting me as it fell. "What in the hell are you shooting at?" A voice behind me, boomed. Startled, I turned, it was George. He had come up with a load of food. I had to explain everything as we hiked toward the Overhang.

Loosing no time, we hurried to the hole. Betty, excited, trying to keep up, George began inserting the long vine into the hole; having to rotate it constantly. Finally, reaching the end, he could feel no resistance. Slowly, pulling the long eighty foot vine out, there was nothing but dirt and a few animal hairs attached to the bark.

George then said, "Excuse me, Betty, I need to pull off my undershirt." "Go ahead, George. I'm used to looking at a man's bare skin," as she punched me. George removed his shirt and undershirt. He wrapped the undershirt around the end of the vine, securing it with one of his shoe laces. Again, slowly rotating the vine as he shoved it into the opening, he gently worked it ever forward. Finally, the end! Slowly retrieving the vine, it seemed ages until the end appeared.

The undershirt was a filth of black dirt. Staring to remove the dirty garment, a beautiful quartz arrow point dropped away from the cloth. Staring, speechless, George picked up the point and rotating it between his fingers, "there's an Indian cave in there." He whispered. "There's something else", I said, picking a small triangular piece of broken emerald and handing it to George. "My charm, it might have come from this very cave." He said.

"Buck, you old rascal, if it hadn't been for you, we would never have found this cave", as I hugged his shaggy neck. We went back to the Overhang and talked for ages about the discovery.

CHAPTER V

Changing Directions

Knowing that the cave had once held human activity, was intriguing to all of us, especially George. Announcing that he would spend the morrow trying to find further evidence, he left for the Norton place, planning to return with some burlap bag cloth. "This rough material wrapped around the long vine should gather more evidence than my undershirt", he laughed. As for me, I had more important things to do. My immediate plans were twofold; to extract enough emeralds in order to pay for developing a mine and to determine if their location held that potential. Early tomorrow, I would go across the mountain and begin work.

Lieutenant had followed Fred from New York to Wilmington and there had found out the Butler's name and address through their car's license plate. Also observing Fred and the Butlers at First Merchants Bank, he had deduced that there must be some connection between Barnes and the Butlers.

Spreading a North Carolina road map, Lieutenant consulted it's town and city index; there it was, Cashiers! Cursing under his breath, at its' distance from Wilmington, He traced a prospective route. From Wilmington to Raleigh, on to Greensboro, hence to Asheville. From Asheville then to Sylva, the county seat for Jackson County. Highway #70 from Durham to Asheville was a single lane road, with no by-passes; it would be a long drive to Sylva. "Better lay over in Asheville the first day," he muttered.

First calling his Director in New York, Lieutenant the headed towards Raleigh and then on to Greensboro, where he stopped for lunch. The area from Greensboro to Morganton along #70 was one vast industrial complex of furniture plants, but this was also the most frustrating lap of the trip.

Lieutenant checked into the Biltmore Hotel in Asheville and after showering, he headed for the tap room. While on a specifics assignment, drinking was sparse and used only as a tool; for instance, to make it easy to enter a conversation with a stranger, in order to obtain information.

The bar-room was beginning to fill up; Lieutenant selected a table next to three khaki-clad men, wearing engineers' boots. He figured they might be highway or mining engineers. Sipping the drink occasionally, for it would be his only one tonight, he could catch drifts of conversation from the near table. As they "got deeper in their drinks", it was easier to follow the men's talk. Good luck! They were discussing mining corundum in Macon County. Corundum is a very hard mineral, used extensively as an abrasive.

Lieutenant leaned closer to the next table and catching the eye of the nearest men, he uttered "pardon me sir, but I couldn't help but overhear your conversation, could I ask a question?" "Why sure sir, slide your chair over and join us." The man invited. Lieutenant introduced himself and said that he was going to Jackson County to look at some mountain land and wondered what kind of minerals were found there. "Well sir, just about every kind of gem, including ruby , aquamarine, beryl, corundum, emerald, sapphire, you name it." "Are you interested in mining property?" The men wanted to know. "Well, not exactly," Lieutenant answered, "I'm with a northern land investment company, I suppose if my people purchased some land with valuable minerals on it, they probably would mine it." "Could you mention the name of your company?" The men were eager to know. "I'm sorry, the company rules forbid it, but if you gentlemen will give me your business cards, it's possible that we might want to consult you in the future." The men eagerly showered Lieutenant with their cards; they had revealed what he was after, so there are emeralds in Jackson County! He thanked the groups and excused himself. It had been a long day!

The road from Asheville to Sylva wound in and out of valleys, sandwiched between high mountains. Lieutenant hadn't been in this part of the south before; it was really quite beautiful and he wished that some one else were driving so he could enjoy more of the scenery.

The courthouse in Sylva was not hard to find; situated in the west end of town, one had to admire its' location for it was elevated, reminding one of a Christmas tree star. Undoubtedly, it is one of North Carolina's most outstanding courthouses!

Lieutenant parked and found the Registrar of Deeds office. Attended by two portly middle aged women, they immediately asked if they could be of help. Smiling and turning on his usual charms, "Yes, mam, I'm doing some legal work for Robert and Betty Butler, and would like a copy of their land deeds for Jackson County and could I get a location map?" Lieutenant asked. "Why, yes sir, if you'll give me a minute." The nearest woman answered, then she left. Just then, another customer walked in and while the second woman was busy, Lieutenant studied the surroundings , in the meantime.

Shortly, the first lady re-appeared , "there are two deeds. That will be two dollars." As she wrote him a receipt. "You will have to get a map from the Tax Assessor's office, it's down the hall." Lieutenant thanked her and left to find the office. "Tax Assessor" it read in gold letters. In here, he would obtain two sizable maps, covering one very large tract of land and a smaller one, representing a lot in Cashiers.

As it was nearing lunch time, he stopped at the Coffee Shop on Main Street, where looking over the lunch menu, country style steak and vegetables were selected. As he waited to be served, his eyes swept the surroundings. On the walls were memorabilia, dating back even to the 1920s. Early diners coming in appeared to be local working people. "What plain looking people, these are." He thought. I bet they have never been out of North Carolina."

Shortly, two rather large, young men entered, dark complexioned, straight, jet black hair and dressed in hunting clothes. He thought they were probably Cherokee Indians. They selected a booth across from him and he noted that in a casual manner, their eyes were continually searching the surroundings. "Damn, I'd hate to run into these jokers in the dark." He thought.

Shortly, the waitress appeared with his order. The food was surprisingly good, he had never eaten country style steak before and the mashed potatoes just melted in his mouth! Subconsciously, he was aware that the two Indians were occasionally glancing his way and he felt somewhat uncomfortable. Finishing the meal, he headed down #107 towards Cashiers.

According to the tax map, the large Butler tract was a few miles out of Glenville, approached from #281, as it branched off #107. Lieutenant drove east on #281, all the time trying to survey the numerous dirt roads that led off to the northeast from #281. The large Butler land must be somewhere in the maze of high mountains, but where? Well, this is as close as I can get without hiring a guide, and that would attract attention. He continued on to a river bridge, then turned around and headed back to #107. Once again on #107, he drove through Cashiers.

As he approached the intersection of #102 and #64, he noted a country store with a large sign, "Betty's Fine Jewelry. Moving west along #64, Mike's Service Station appeared on the right; Lieutenant stopped here to get gas and seek information.

No sooner than Lieutenant had pulled up to the gas pump than a young man, obviously the mechanic appeared, munching on a sandwich. He asked how much gas Lieutenant wanted. "Fill her up and listen, I'm a cousin of Bob Butler, could you tell where he lives in Cashiers?" "Why, yes, you just passed it, it's the country store, up at the intersection." "You mean sir, they live in a store?" Lieutenant was surprised. "Yes, but they recently bought a large boundary of land with a house on it; I'd expect they are over there, working on it." "Well thank you, I guess I'll have to see them next time." Lieutenant paid for the fill up and drove back to the country store.

Parking in front, he could see no cars under the shed, so he walked up on the porch and knocked on the door. There was no response to repeated knocks, so he peeped through the large glass window on his left. All he could discern was a large flat top desk with various small tools scattered about the top. "This must be her work shop." He decided. Still seeing no sign of life, He walked around back, a huge pile of firewood under a shed, large scattered trees, nothing much of interest.

He turned and started to the small back porch, then stopped suddenly; "what's this?" he thought. A pile of gravel sized pebbles, next to a chair, seemed odd. They must have been broken up for some reason; perhaps they must be connected to the woman's jewelry business, he decided. A larger flat stone, near, looked as if it had recently been worked on. Picking it up, he saw a long depression, where something had been pried out; the depression had three sides. "Well, this could be important; I'll just take it for a souvenir for study; after all, doesn't an emerald have six sides, this depression had three!"

Lieutenant headed toward Asheville, where he would turn in the rental car to the agency company from Wilmington. After calling the Director, he would board a train to New York.

Each morning, for the next five days, I would eat a hurried breakfast and be off to the other side, as soon as it got light enough to see the trail. The August summer mornings were calm, it was the afternoons that were to be aware of, for the storms were now the norm, not the exceptions.

It seemed that there was a storm in progress, in one direction or another. I had made good progress for four days and had escaped a storm by the skin of my teeth; usually by heeding it's early warnings. On the fifth day, I was not so fortunate.

This day, I had reached the work site earlier than usual, hoping to finish the week's work and return to camp early. Already it was quitting time, but the chunk of rock in my hands had already yielded two stunning crystals and despite rumblings to the west, I was determined to see if there were more jewels in the piece.

Working furiously, I was unaware of how close the impending storm was until suddenly a sharp crack, some hundred yards above, jolted me into reality. Quickly stashing the tools, and wrapping the day's crystals, I lost no time heading for the trail leading to the top of the pass, and if I missed it, I might well wander over thousands of acres in the fading light.

At last, the trail came into sight, and if I could at least beat the coming storm to the top of the pass, I could at least stay on the path. The half-mile to the top was covered in record time, and when it was reached, I paused not for a second, but continued plunging down.

Within three or four minutes, I was deep in the pass when the storm struck. Gale sized winds and blinding sheets of rain, totally engulfed me and visibility was limited to a dozen yards or less. Desperately, I searched for a large boulder to hover against, and finding one, lay down as close to it as possible. Rivulets of water rushed by my face, compounding the misery brought on by a drenched body.

The storm continued unabated, seeming never to end, and now

it was dark. Finally, after an hour it passed on. I got to my feet and continued, but at a snail's pace; at least the well-worn trail could be followed. Reaching the large boulders that I usually skirted, this time, throwing caution aside, I plunged between them and continued on.

At last the sound of the falls above the pool could be heard, and reaching there, turned east toward camp. A few minutes later, a faint glow ahead, and shortly I staggered into camp, more like a half-drowned rat than a human.

Betty grabbed me, wet clothes and all, hugging and sobbing. She had been frantic with worry, not knowing whether I had been struck, or lost in the wilderness. She handed me a drink and began stripping the wet clothes away, then drying me from head to foot, thrust warm, dry clothes in my hands. Shivering like a freezing dog, I moved close to the fire. Shortly, with dry clothes, a warm fire, a soothing drink, and above all, a loving wife, my spirits returned.

Now, in a calmer setting, we could review the last five days. Counting the week's take, I had extracted 70 crystals, and hopefully, these would bring us enough to develop a mine. "It's really necessary to develop a mine?" Betty asked. "Can't we just go on like this, extracting the emeralds, after all, we can live on what we have already." "No, honey, it wouldn't work that way; this thing is too big, and the only way to protect it, is an organization. Without an organization, its' location would be found, and you and I could not protect it." "I never thought of it in that way." Betty admitted. "I know honey, just imagine for a second if this place was discovered, there would be crazy rock hounds crawling all over the place; we would be forced to keep an armed guard there night and day. Just as soon as we can put enough money in the bank, we have to begin forming a group to develop and protect our property.

Next morning, we started down to the Norton house; last evenings storm had saturated the countryside, leaving one with the impression of being inside a steaming green house. We heard hammering as we neared the house and true to form, George was working on the flooring.

"Well, I see you survived the storm; it was even strong down here." George greeted us. I then proceeded to relate my own nightmare with the storm. "By the way, be sure to stop by Mike's when you get to Cashiers, you've had some telephone calls." He reminded me.

We stopped by Mike's before going home. "The telephone company wants you to call them, and the flooring company in Rosman has called twice." Mike said. At once, I called Sylva and the phone company said they would come tomorrow if we were ready.

Galloway answered when I called Rosman, "Mr. Butler, if you want the property, I will take ninety thousand for it; that is my bottom price." I hesitated a few seconds, then told him to put his lawyer on searching the record and writing the deed, also I asked for some maps of the property. "I'll be down to close this as soon as I hear from you." "I'll put the lawyer on it at once, shouldn't take over a day or two." Galloway advised.

"Well, which way to go?" I asked my wife. "I need to take the stones to Fred, but the Galloway land will be ready in a couple of days, and that's important. The phone people are coming in the morning. "Bob, I don't feel good about you driving alone to Wilmington with a fortune, take George with you." Betty seemed very concerned. "Yeah, I'll talk to George about it; it's really not a good idea to even call Fred that we're coming."

Almost before we could finish breakfast next morning, the phone people showed up. They needed to run a short line from across the road to the store; this, they started on first. The latest thing in telephones were the dial type, Betty selected the color. In two hours time, the phone was in operation. I had to poke fun at Betty; she started to call everyone in Cashiers!

Two days later, I called Rosman early in the morning and Galloway said to come on down, the deed was ready. George was still at the Norton place, so I drove to Rosman, alone. Meantime, I told Betty to drive to the Norton place and tell George to be ready early tomorrow to go with me to Wilmington. Betty had to drive the Jeep, which she wasn't too happy with, but after all, I had the longer drive to Rosman.

The flooring plant was humming with full production; a crescendo from planers, resaws and the main saw, engulfed one like an out-of-tune orchestra. Exposed to such noise as this for eight hours, and five days a week, must undoubtedly leave the listener with a certain disposition!

Galloway and his lawyer were waiting when I entered the office and the signing took only a couple of minutes. The lawyer would meet me next morning in Sylva to have the deed recorded. I asked Galloway if I could use his forester to help with the boundary lines, if necessary, and he assured me he would. Also, he asked me to be on the lookout for good quality red and white oak boundaries of timber.

Next morning, George came by, prepared to go with me to Wilmington, but I had to meet the lawyer in Sylva at ten o'clock, and we would leave in the morning. George was elated when I told him about buying the large Galloway property, "don't have time to talk about it now, but we'll have all day to discuss it going to Wilmington." "Be sure to bring a side arm and your shotgun tomorrow; I'll have a 9mm Browning with me." Shortly, I left for Sylva.

At ten, I met Galloway's lawyer and he had the deed, dually recorded. "Mr. Butler, you've made one hell of a buy! That land is probably worth three times what you paid for it." The lawyer said. "Then, why did the company sell it?" I wanted to know. "Well, they want to expand their production and desperately needed the money; you just caught them at the right time." I thanked the man and asked for his business card.

Today was Friday, payday for the sawmill, and I was certain that Fred would be there. It was safer not to call him beforehand, for there was no telling how many people in New York that Fred had unwittingly might have aroused interest in the source of the emeralds, when he tried to sell them.

We took the usual route down to South Carolina, then eastward toward the coast. At Charlotte, four hours later, we stopped at a drive in, but did not get out, eating the lunch in the car, and then taking turns going to the bath room, never for a second leaving the precious cargo unattended!

During the morning part of the trip, we talked about the Galloway tract. I asked George if he had hunted over much of it. "no, not very much, only in the lower reaches, where the hardwoods were more prominent, in the higher elevations you'll find hemlock, white pine and red spruce; not much food value in those types. My father remembered the vast chestnut groves in the lower elevations; he said those woods were full of turkey, deer and bear. But you know in the higher elevations, I doubt if anyone living today could tell you what's up there." "Well, George, someday you and I are going to find out." I predicted. "Bob, that tract is at least more than twice the size of the Norton land."

We rolled into Wilmington at three o'clock and went straight to the mill; Fred was in the office and when we walked in, almost fell out of his chair with surprise. "What the heck! Where did you come from?" He blurted. "We didn't want to telegraph our coming, just wanted to play it safe. Here is a valuable cargo" as I placed the box of crystals before him. Fred went to the door and told his secretary that he wanted privacy.

Opening the box, he exhaled a long breath as he viewed its' contents. Finally, he spread out the stones and studied them intently. "Whew!" He uttered. "I'll have to call New York and leave Monday." He said. Placing the lot in the huge safe. "Wells Fargo will have to take these up, no way that I can personally deliver them; I'll have them come out in the morning, so they can be there by Tuesday. "We drove to the Barnes' residence on Oleander and Rachel was impressed with George; she kept asking him questions about his people. "I'm so thrilled to have a full blood Cherokee Indian as a guest." It was quite evident that George was somewhat embarrassed.

That evening, we dined in Wilmington, down on the waterfront. Since we had come without first calling, Rachel had already been committed to a prior engagement with her club, so she was unable to join us. This suited the occasion, for now we could talk business. Someday, Rachel would have to be made aware of what was going on; that is, when we were finally organized and the mine protected.

Expansion on the Wilmington airport had just been completed and now Fred could take the Piedmont Airline flight to New York. No more over night trains would Fred have to endure! "I can take the seven o'clock flight, be in New York by nine and with luck, conduct business and be back in Wilmington by nine, the same evening." Fred bragged.

"So, tell me about the large tract of land you just closed on." Fred wanted to know. "Did you find more emeralds on it?" "No Fred, I bought it for additional security around the mine and it's got lots of timber on it; but God only knows what else is on it!" I reminded Fred that this trip to New York would probably be his most important, for the results would determine whether we would have the money to develop the mine. Fred understood that it was on his shoulders and he was highly apprehensive about it. "Well Fred, you did an excellent job on your first trip; I have complete confidence in you." I assured him. "I wish you two would stay over until Monday, it would have such a soothing effect on my nerves; would you?" "Fred, as much as we would like to, there is just too much back in Jackson County, that has to be taken care of." With that, I could sense that Fred understood our urgency, as he sighed, shaking his head in resignation.

While we ate, George was fascinated by the ship that had just passed by; it was the first one that he had seen since disembarking a troop ship in World War I!

We left for Cashiers next morning after enjoying a breakfast, midst a surrounding of linen, silverware and flowers. Orange juice, a tropical fruit mixture, followed by scrambled eggs, grits and home fries – and not toast! But, thin crusty freshly baked biscuits! For what ever faults that Rachel ever possessed, she was one hell of a cook!

Leaving our host on the driveway, waving their goodbyes and tooting my horn in response, we left for Cashiers.

Saturday morning at nine o'clock, Fred met with Wells Fargo at the mill, where the box of emeralds was picked up and sent to Finklestein & Finklestein in New York. At least, Fred would not be walking around this time with a fortune in his boots!

As soon as the airport expansion in Wilmington was completed, Piedmont Airlines established a terminal there. They were using a "day coach" version of the Douglas DC-3. The military version was known as the C-47; a tried and true airplane used in WWII for transporting troops and supplies.

Fred nestled comfortably in his plush seat, stared at the changing patterns below, as the rising sun began to transform patches of darkness into shade of light. He had departed at seven and expected to land at nine; a two-hour flight, Piedmont promised. Unlike viewing from a train window, the scenery below was changing far more rapidly, and shortly the large expanse of pine forests gave way to more open farmland. Eventually, everything gave way to haze shrouded city conglomerate as the plane purred northward.

For the past half hour, Fred had been dozing and was suddenly jolted awake by the pilots' announcement that they would land in fifteen minutes. It had seemed to Fred that they had taken off just a few minutes ago! My! How things are changing, he mused!

The plane touched smoothly at LaGuardia, and a line of cabs were waiting as Fred entered one and he only had to utter – the "Waldorf".

Since he expected to conclude the business and catch the seven o'clock flight back, Fred intended not to check into the hotel, but to learn when the latest check-in time would be if that became necessary.

"That will be one o'clock sir." The clerk answered, "may I hold a reservation for you?" "No, I'll wait until one and call you." As Fred headed for the dining room, the desk clerk immediately placed a call, "he's not checking in, just now, maybe at one o'clock." "I think he's going to the dining room." "Thank you, if things change, call me." Was the reply.

Fred ordered orange juice, coffee and two donuts, his appointment was twenty-five minutes away, but he could walk the distance in five minutes, so he waited patiently for the order. Presently, it arrived and he sipped, munched and contemplated the coming events.

As usual, the Finklestein brothers were happy to see Fred; they had continually called, asking for more gems. Wells Fargo had delivered the box on Saturday, but it was not yet opened, now it was sitting on Joseph's desk.

After the usual introductory greetings and small talks were finished, they opened the box. The bill of laden said, "70 emeralds", but the Finklesteins were not prepared to view such a sight! They gasped, they sighed, they coughed – such a sight! "Fred, it will take us a week to place a value and an offer on these." Joseph and Aaron agreed. "You mean, based on the average of the first ones that I bought up, you can't go on that?" "No, Fred, you must understand that each stone must be placed under a light and studies intensely, among other tests." Aaron emphasized. "Well, I had intended for Rubin & Son to have twenty of these, can you call Wells Fargo and have them deliver them to them?" "As you wish." Joseph said, now, you select the ones for them." "Well, they look all the same to me." And counted the twenty, putting them back in the box.

By the time that Fred had reached Rubin& Son, the stones had been delivered. They hadn't expected Fred before two o'clock, but were delighted by his early appearance. Initial greetings over, he was led into the main office and invited to sit. He had remembered how expansively and lavishly laid out the office was; gold everywhere, mahogany, red leather, paintings, the works!

The jewels were spread on Rubin's desk as the usual oohs and ahs followed, at their sight. Rubin's technician appeared and after that it would take at least two or more days to determine their value. "We had expected a larger shipment." Rubin. said. "When can you send us more?" "I had to divide the lot between you and the Finklesteins." Fred reminded him. "I'll try my best, but it will be at least thirty days." Fred received a receipt for the lot and hailing a cab, headed for the airport.

As George and I drove back to Cashiers, we kept on the subject of the big Galloway tract. "If you cleared the old tram way, you could put in a good road, which would reach almost to the pass." George pointed out. "It has a five percent grade, which allowed the small logging engines to reach most of the chestnut timber in the late eighteen hundreds, even as late as the 1920's. From where it would end, it would only be around 12 or 1500 feet to your mine site." "That's a thought, George, but it would be beyond reason to reach the mine site with a road." "We'll, put in a simple overhead cable system, that would not be hard to do!" "George, you've got your thinking cap on, that's a great idea, let's go over and talk to Frank Holden. We'll try to catch him tomorrow."

Betty was waiting for us with supper when we reached Cashiers. While we were eating, she said that when she stopped at Mike's Service Station, some man had stopped by,. asking where we lived, said he was related to us." "Well, I wouldn't know who that could possibly be. " I said. "Did Mike describe what he looked like?" "He said that he had black curly hair and was rather dark complexioned." "Well there are no relations of mine like that are dark complexioned; could it be one of your nephews, George?" "My nephews? No way any Cherokee with curly hair, would not be considered full blood." George seemed taken by surprise at my question and I regretted blurting it out.

The Galloway land just purchased, cornered with out Norton land on the large stream, below the bridge. From here, it followed the stream for one mile, hence it crossed our road and continued in an eastward direction for another mile to a huge inscribed boulder. From the boulder, it took a northern course, crossing the mountain and into the valley floor. Here, it joined the Holden property on a stone corner; hence it turned west, following the Holden line for two miles to another stone corner. From here, it turned south along Holden's line to my wire fence corner, continuing along my Norton line, crossing the mountain and down to the beginning stone corner on the creek. The land was two miles wide by seven miles long, containing some 8,960 acres, more or less.

George stopped by next morning in his pick-up truck and we drove over to the Holden's. They lived at Glenville, just off #107. You had to cross a branch of the beautiful Tuskaseegee River on an old iron bridge; the Holden house sat on a low hill, facing the bridge, two storied with a large porch and surrounded by ancient white pines. It would surely be an artist's inspiration!

To our left was a huge red barn with several utility buildings off to the side; sounds of iron banging against iron led us in that direction. Heavy equipment. Bulldozers, front-end loaders and all manner of machinery parked around, seemed to beckon "please come on awaken us!"

Following the sounds, we found Frank Holden walking around a D-6 bulldozer, two men were installing pins and bushings on tracks of the machine. Frank stopped and greeted us, and led us to the outside, where the noise was less intrusive. I apologized for not calling beforehand, but Frank always the genial person, laughed, "I was just getting in their way, they know what they're doing."

We sat on a long bench beside the building and I opened up by telling Frank about buying the Galloway land. Surprised, he laughed, "What on earth made you buy that rock pile?" "Frank, I ask myself that question, maybe it's because I never saw a tract of land that I didn't like." "Well. I can tell you this, it's got a lot of rock on it; what do you plan to do with it?" "Well, Frank, that's what I came over to talk to you about; I want to clear the old tram road and turn it into a road, that at least a 4X4 truck can use; you know the grade had to be much less than ten percent for a steam engine to climb." "Yes, that's true. As a boy, I remember when they were logging the place with a steam engine and horses and mules. Why, I've seen chestnut logs, four feet in diameter loaded on the rail cars coming off that mountain." Frank seemed to re-live his childhood as he remembered the time.

"Well, Frank, you've had more experience building mountain roads than anyone else around here, that's why I came to you' what do you think?" "Bob, that would be quite a challenge, to say the least. Before giving you an answer, we would have to walk over the old railroad. Are you in a hurry?" "I would like to get it done before winter comes, so

89

the road bed could set, but I want you to do the job, if there's anyway you will take it."

Frank was silent a few minutes, then, "tell you what, let's both walk the old rail bed tomorrow, then, I can give you an answer." We agreed that was the best approach.

When George and I returned to Cashiers, Betty said that Fred had called and for me to call him as soon as I came in. George agreed to go with Frank and I tomorrow, and would come by early for me. Placing the call to Fred, his secretary answered, saying that Fred was out in the mill; it was a full two minutes before he came on. "Bob, it's going to be three or four days before the people in New York can complete the work, then, I'll have to go back up. "Well, how long was your flight; how long did it take?" I was curious to know. Oh! It was great and only took two hours; no more six hour train trips for me." Fred chuckled. "You and Betty be prepared to come to Wilmington after I come back from the next trip." "Thanks, we'll wait to hear from you", I said, "hope it's good news."

Next morning, Frank, Tommy Holden, George and I started at the Galloway Holden corner. The logging operations were discontinued in 1920, at the time that the great chestnut blight had decimated this magnificent tree. Quality chestnut logs were sent to the lumber mill, while poor quality material was sent to be ground up, where the acid extracted, then the grindings made into paper.

We figured that railroad bed to be on a 5% grade, which we about the maximum grade that a steam engine could climb, while pulling three or four logging cars. Timber along the road bed was only some twenty-five years old, so would not be hard to push up; Frank was pleased with this. Yellow poplar and white pine were larger than other species because they grew faster.

After half a mile, the road bed reversed itself and ran westward, ever climbing. By the time we had reached the end, we had climbed over two thousand feet. I pointed out to Frank where I wanted a parking space that could be excavated, fortunately, the spot was at the top of a ridge, which was fairly level.

We sat for a long while and talked, Frank pointed out, that the trees would have to be felled and pushed off the right of way, before any excavating could begin; the stumps would have to be left high enough, so the bulldozer could push them out of the ground. Instead of retracing our climb, we left the road bed and went straight down the mountain. When we returned to the Holden place, Frank said that he would have to do some figuring; then he would call me.

A gentle breeze swept up the mountain side; entering the pass it set the leaves of the stunted hardwoods to twittering, swaying the towering conifers to and fro, swirling in and out of nooks and cranny's, until it woke the Keeper. He had spent much of the hot summer in temporary quarters, under the large boulders in the pass. The ground and gray squirrels were easy prey, but they didn't entirely satisfy his enormous appetite, now he desired a change of menu!

As the morning sun crept up the pass, warming the morning's coolness. Keeper poked his head from under the large boulder; testing the air currents, no dangers from below were detected, he cautiously slid into the trail and slid down the mountain.

His destination was the apple orchard, above the Norton house. Although most of the apples did not ripen for another two months, many trees were shedding faulty fruit, which attracted large and small animals and birds. He desired a fat, juicy meal; perhaps a plump ground hog or rabbit. A hefty meal of one of these would satisfy his cravings for a couple of weeks.

Turning right at the waterfall, he passed the Overhang camp and then chose a slanting downward course to the long white oak ridge; from here it was an easy path to the orchard. He would hunt at his own pleasure and at night sleep under nearby rock overhangs.

When George and I left the Holdens, after the trek up the old logging right of way, Betty was waiting to tell me that Fred had called to New York. That was good news, I hoped, for if all went well, we could begin to work on developing the mine.

Catching the seven o'clock Piedmont flight to New York, Fred Barnes settled comfortably in his seat and contemplated on the coming meetings. He was more confident now, with some experience from the other trip; at the same time however, this was a much bigger deal and he couldn't help but keep his thoughts off the coming meetings.

As per schedule, the plane landed on time and shortly he was in a cab headed for the Waldorf. Fred glanced at his watch, he had forty=five minutes to make the Finklestein appointment, plenty of time to check by the hotel to find out check in time and to reserve a room, if that becomes necessary.

Entering the Waldorf-Astoria was like entering Grand Central, with people rushing to and fro, like ants. Striding to the desk with his small overnight bag, he inquired about the latest he could check in. "That will be two o'clock, Mr. Barnes." The clerk responded. Fred was shocked that the clerk remembered his name from the first trip and he said, "that's amazing, you remembered me." "Oh, I have a good memory, I meet so many nice people; I find that most people appreciate their names being remembered." The clerk smiled. The clerk had good reason to remember Fred's name; it would mean a nice reward, after making a phone call. "Can I check my bag temporarily until I find out if I'm going to stay?" Fred asked. "Why certainly, sir, I'll take care of that." The clerk said, smiling, he stored the bag and gave Fred a receipt.

Leisurely, Fred walked up 5th Avenue, weaving in and out of the morning's rush, and unaware that he was being followed. Entering Finklestein & Finklestein, he was greeted and ushered into the office.

Joseph and Aaron greeted him warmly, for both brothers were very fond of Fred; after all, had he not sold them valuable emeralds, at a price far below those from Columbia?

Joseph opened the conversation by saying the recent batch of stones were of very good quality and overall were pleased with them. Opening an envelope, he spread some papers on the desk. "Now, Fred, the 50 stones averaged 500 karats each, or 25,000 total, at $50 a karat, we offer you $1,250,000 for the lot." "Well, Joseph, I trust that you have put your best figure on their value?" "Yes, we have, Fred, Aaron spent a week placing a value on them." Joseph nodded. "Well, then, I accept the price; wire the amount to my bank in Wilmington." Fred felt comfortable with the offer.

"Now, Fred, there is something important that I want you to carefully consider," Joseph said. "And that is?" Fred was surprised.

"You and your group apparently are approaching the time that you will be large operators in this business, and if this happens, you can almost count on crossing the path of organized criminals." "Well, I hadn't thought about that," Fred shook his head, "the region where my group operates doe not have such criminal elements." "Fred, I'm speaking of groups in New York, or elsewhere; you going to sell your product in large cities, where such criminals operate." Joseph continued. "In these surroundings is where you are exposed, then they will follow you to your source." "Well, that sounds like something that we should be concerned about then; what do you suggest that we do?" "I hope you don't get the impression that Aaron and I are trying to sell you a bill of goods, but it once happened to us, until I consulted a friend and he suggested we make a contribution to the coming state of Israel. As such, we came under the protection of the Mossad, their intelligence branch. When the criminal group that threatened us were warned, they fled like dogs with their tails between their legs." Joseph laughed.

"Then, you're suggesting that we make a contribution; but how much would that be?" Fred was concerned. "I strongly suggest it and I would say $10,000," Joseph nodded to Fred. "For the time being, take $10,000 from your payment of these stones, which will represent a part of my commission." "Meantime, I will urge my group to make a contribution." Fred said.

Joseph nodded in the affirmative, pulled out a golden certificate and had Fred to sign it. "You will eventually receive a golden badge with the letter "M" in its' center." He said, "Congratulations, Fred." They shock hands. "I do this because I trust you, Joseph." Fred said. "The feeling is mutual, my friend." Joseph answered.

It was nearing twelve o'clock and Fred hurried on to Rubin & Son, two blocks away. They were pleased to see him, but somewhat disappointed to receive only twenty stones. The value of these amounted to $435,000. This was somewhat less per stone than what Fred had received from Finklesteins and he did not hesitate to express his disappointment.

Leaving Rubin & Son, Fred stopped by the Waldorf, retrieved his bag and took a cab to the airport. Here, he would wait for the two o'clock flight to Wilmington.

Next morning, after we had made the climb up an old logging right of way, Frank Holden called, "Bob, the least I can put a road bed up the mountain is $25,000. I can put four men cutting the trees and a D-4 tractor pushing the logs and tops off the side. The sawyers can cut any merchantable logs and pile them for the sawmill. You will have to arrange to pull the good logs." "How long do you figure it will take to cut the trees?" I asked. "Probably two weeks, but I can put two D-6 tractors behind the cutters after the first week. If we have good weather, I can complete the road in thirty days." Frank sounded confident over the phone. "That sounds good to me; when can you start?" I was anxious to know. "In a day or so, as soon as I can round up some cutters." Frank assured me.

Fred called as soon as he had returned to Wilmington; he wanted Betty and I to come down. "Betty has to stay and look after things; I'm having a road under construction, among other things. George is busy on the Norton house; it'll just be me." I told him.

Betty rose early next morning, dressing in khaki pants and shirt, then, pulling on her hiking boots, she fixed a hearty breakfast. Today she planned to stop by the Holden's then go to the Galloway tract where Holden's men were clearing the right of way.

Packing enough lunch for her and Buck, she backed the Jeep from under the shed and headed towards Glenville. Her knapsack not only contained a lunch, but also the trusty 9 mm Browning automatic, which she always carried in the woods.

Crossing the iron bridge, she stopped by the Holden house and chatted with Frank's wife, Bessie, for a few minutes. "Frank and Tommie were on the mountain with their crew; your husband wants the road finished in thirty days and Frank is determined to meet the deadline." Bessie said.

Leaving the Holden place, Betty continued on towards the mountain. As she neared the work site, a continuance roar of falling trees, power saws and a bulldozer, all mingled together, reminded her of an approaching thunderstorm. Parking the Jeep and shouldering the knapsack, she warned Buck to stay close to her side. "If a tree hits you, it'll mash more of you than toe nails."

Frank was standing near the bulldozer as it pushed treetops off the right of way. Greeting Betty, he explained what was going on. "The trees are cut, leaving high stumps, so the larger tractors could more easily push them out of the ground." "I've split the new crews up so they won't get in each other's way; the forward crew is separated from the lower crew by a block of timber. Also, we are piling the good logs, so you can sell them to a sawmill." Betty told him that she was going to hike up the mountain. "Well, be careful not to be caught in a thunderstorm up there; it you hear any thunder in the distance, you'd head back down." Frank cautioned. "I will be careful." Betty assured him. Carefully staying out of range of falling trees, she and Buck started the climb.

Fred was behind his desk when I reached the mill around two o'clock. After greetings, he outlined the details of his trip. The Finklestein sale brought $1,240,000 and the Rubin & Son, $435,000. "Now, Bob, I was cautioned in the strongest terms by Joseph Finklestein, that as we expand in this business, we are very likely to cross paths with organized crime." "I would expect that we will, Fred; anytime there is an accumulation of wealth, you know that criminals are bound to be hanging around." "So what did Finklestein suggest we do before hand?" "Bob, he urged me to contribute to the coming state of Israel, and as such, we could fall under the protection of their Mossad. I took the liberty of contributing $10,000 from my commission in the latest sale." He also suggested that I talk to you about doing the same." "Fred, I'll have to give that some thought, right now, it's going to take a lot of money to develop the mine." "Another thing, Bob, both Finklestein and Rubin are fully loaded with our emeralds, and to sell more in the near future, we will have to go to auction. The auction is held in October for the coming Christmas season and again in spring, for the summer season." "Well, Fred, that's up to you to get the details; you've got to let us know well ahead of time."

Broom sedge in the orchard had by now reached its' maximum height, fully matured. The lower parts of it's stems were beginning to take on a hue of beige, intermingled with summer green, a sure sign that fall was just around the corner.

Keeper, well concealed by the tall grass, slid quietly towards a large apple tree loaded with fruit. Surely there must be dozens of faulty apples on the ground, inviting the local populace to dine! Sure enough, Keeper would not be disappointed for there was movement just ahead, as he paused at the base of the tree. Well, camouflaged, he could easily pass for a dead limb.

Two rabbits were munching on the fallen fruit; but what was a rabbit? Nothing but a large head and loose skin covering a stack of bones. No layers of juicy fat here! The big snake wanted a thick layered woodchuck, fat, juicy; something more to his liking.

He decided to move on. Usually a ground hog will feed not too far from its' den, so if frightened, it will streak to safety. Where would the most likely encounter might take place? Of course, the fruit trees on the edge of the orchard, next to the woods. He headed in that direction.

Moving to the edge of the orchard Keeper found a well-laden apple tree, a slick path leading into the nearby woods from the tree, indicated that the area was frequently visited. Keeper would patiently wait here and let his meal come to him.

From the first week in August to the first week in September, the Holden crew had worked ten hours a day on the road, now it was finished. Frank had put in several culverts, servicing the drainage ditch on the upper sides of the road. Water bars, spaced at regular intervals, would prevent heavy rains from washing the road. Without the drainage ditch and the water bars the road would only last until the first heavy rain.

At the end of the road, the crew had leveled a parking space, large enough to accommodate four large timber trucks. After the grading was completed, a heavy bulldozer, a D-8, was run up and down the roadbed, packing it firmly. Frank Holden had performed a professional job, and for his efforts, I paid him a $5,000 bonus on top of the $25,000 contract. Needless to say that he was well pleased and assured me that he would like to do business with me in the future.

Betty, Buck and myself got in the Jeep and drove up the new road. It was a bit rough, due to the heavy bulldozer tracks, but we didn't mind! Now, I could work longer hours at the mine site. I could sleep at home and enjoy a hot meal. No more camping out or having to walk a long distance, just to get to work!

CHAPTER VI

Mining Green Fire

"**B**etty if we're to develop the mine, Frank Holden must be brought in now, for he and his sons are the group that I think would be the most dependable. We can't lie in bed at night worrying about some outside group to work the mine, not knowing their background, nor anything about them. As I see this thing, I think it must be a family situation, some one that we know first hand." "I know Bob, it concerns me, I've been thinking the same thing; at least we can trust Frank Holden and his family." Betty nodded in agreement.

That evening, I called Frank and he agreed to go with Betty and me on the mountain.

Early next morning, we took the jeep and drove to Glenville; Frank was waiting when we pulled up. Betty graciously relinquished her front seat and she and Buck rode in back. This way, Frank and I could talk, above the noisy vehicle.

The middle of September had ushered in slight changes in color. Under story dogwoods and sourwoods with the shades of red and yellow poplars flaunting their golden leaves; these colors were reminding us that fall was rapidly approaching.

Starting up the new road, I changed into low gear and the little motor responded with a higher pitched whine. Betty and Buck in the rear, were the recipients of the bouncing ride and I tried to go as slow as possible. At the roads end, we parked in the cleared spot and set in silence for a few minutes, drinking in the spectacular view, which extended as far as the eye could reach.

"Frank, we have to walk some twelve hundred feet from here and it's going to be rough going, are you up to it?" I asked. "Lead the way and don't worry about me." He sounded, somewhat irritated.

Threading our way around trees, rocks and rotting logs was hard enough, but the really brutal thing was the steep slope. You had to continually grab hold of a sapling to keep from sliding down the mountain! "Butler, I hope to hell you're not planning to put a road along this God forsaken mountain." Frank rasped. "No, nothing like that, but what I have in mind might surprise you." For the next thirty minutes, we struggled ahead.

At last we came to the mine site and sat down on some rocks for a welcomed reprieve. Frank looked, shaking his head; I was sure that he could discern no difference in this remote place than the area that we had just passed through!

"Frank, I guess it's time that we have a serious talk, I suspect you are wondering why we brought you to this place." "Yes, Bob, I've been dwelling on that subject since we got out of the Jeep; it must be important." "Frank, what I am about to show you must be kept in absolute secret, at least for the time being. Not even your family must know, for the time being." "Bob, I can keep my mouth shut." Unwavering, Frank looked me straight in the eyes.

Going to a flat stone, I lifted it and retrieved a broken emerald that I had secreted previously. Handing it to Frank, he stared at it, turning it over and over. "What is it?" He finally asked. "It's an emerald, the most precious gem on earth." I answered simply. "Then, why did you reveal this to me?" Frank wanted to know. "I want you to work for me, that is, all of your family, when I open a mine here." "First place, Bob, how are you going to service this place. Putting a road in here would be next to impossible. Also, you realize that we make a good living, running heavy equipment and raising cattle. Whatever your offer might be, would have to be mighty attractive." Frank sounded blunt and to the point. "You're right, a road would be out of the question. I plan on an overhead cable system, similar to a ski lift. As far as actually working the mine, that would possibly take one or two days a week, using air or hydraulic tools. Then subtracting the crystals with air tools, would probably take two days a week. We would not be working on a day-to-day basis; we would only be working as orders come in.

You would have to put on a salary." "Well, that sounds like it might work," Frank nodded.

"Next thing, can you and your crew cut a fifty foot right of way from the Jeep to here and get it completed before winter sets in? All that would be required, would be to cut the trees down, leave the logs in place, but move the brush and limbs off area, so they wouldn't impede putting up hangers and the cable. If you can do that, give me a price as soon as you can." "Let me get some figures together and I'll give you a figure in a day or two," Frank answered.

Frank was silent for a long spell, probably hashing over what we had just discussed. I was surprised when he suggested that we drive over to Boone and talk to an engineer who had erected the ski lift there. I had heard of it of course, for it was new and had been all over the news. An overhead cable system must be quite an engineering fete, I thought. "Frank, that's an excellent idea, after all, it's going to take an engineering firm to build this system, let me know when you can go with me to Boone."

There were so many things to do, so many different directions to follow, I simply had to figure out which came first. If Frank was to clear the right of way to the mine site, the right of way had to be marked, so driving to the cleared area next day, I left Betty and Buck in the Jeep and using a hand compass set a straight course toward the mine site, flagging the center line trees.

As luck would have it, when the end was reached, I was below the site by at least two hundred feet. Now, the line would have to be corrected. Starting at the mine site, I steered a course slightly to the right and again flagged the center trees. This time, my luck held. When the end was reached, the cleared area, Jeep, Betty and Buck, and all were right on the compass heading! Now though, I had to go all the way back and take down the flagging tape from the first line, which was incorrect! At least Betty had the foresight to have brought some lunch, for it was well into the afternoon before I finally staggered back. At least that job was completed. Now Frank's crew would have a centerline to follow.

Under story foliage was now in full color and the trees themselves were beginning to take on this hue. First the yellow poplars in the lower altitudes and now the hickories, oaks and maples were joining nature's choir. Fall's bounty was also evident, squirrels were after hickory nuts and acorns; hogs, deer and bear were not only after acorns, but they were also helping themselves to our apples. This I didn't mind so much, but the bears, not satisfied with fruit on the ground, had to climb up in the trees and break the limbs. We had spent considerable time and money, getting the orchard back in shape, and apparently, Mr. Bear wasn't aware of this. We had plenty room for bear skin rugs.

Frank called and said that he could clear the right-of-way for a thousand dollars and it would take about a week with four men, so I told him to go ahead. He also assured me that he would be at the mine site to make sure that none of the work crew would be poking around the area.

In the meantime, Fred called from Wilmington and invited us, including George, to come down for a few days; I thought it a good idea, because we needed to discuss some things relative to our immediate plans for the fall. Apparently, Fred was anxious to find more buyers in New York, even if we didn't plan to enter the fall auction then.

George was all for going with us; I had bragged so much about the beauty of the cypress and tupelo gum trees, especially in the fall; now he wanted to see these for himself. We had a problem however; how would we three, along with Buck ride in a forty Ford coupe? No way, I would drive in the Jeep, and the others would ride in the Ford. It was really time for us to consider buying a larger automobile for such occasions as this and if we found one in Wilmington, then George could drive one of the vehicles back to Cashiers. As a gift to Betty, she would be the one to select the car; often my wife had expressed the wish just to sit behind the wheel of a BMW, to see what it would feel like!

Early Friday morning, George drove up. After parking, he unloaded a leather suitcase and stashed it in the back of the Ford. We were already waiting and ready and he wasted no time hitting the road. Taking the usual #107 south, which pointed to South Carolina, this would be the best, uncongested route to Wilmington. Betty led the way and I followed in the Jeep.

The fall morning in Jackson County was brisk, with even a smathering of frost in the low areas, but as we descended towards the south, warmer air felt more comfortable, at least to me, riding in an open Jeep.

An hour later, we were in the piedmont section of South Carolina, a beautiful red clay area, which had been farmed this during the great depression, by growing cotton. Now, thanks to the post wartime economy, things were bustling along. At Westminester, we turned east on route #123 towards Greenville. It seemed that all along the way, new buildings were going up, not only houses, but factories as well! What a profound change, from the horrid depression days!

By passes around cities and towns were yet to be built, so going through Greenville with it's stop lights slowed us somewhat, but Betty didn't mind, after all, Furman was her Alma Mater! The area from Greenville to Spartanburg was simply bursting with activity.

Charlotte demanded a rest stop for us, for stop light after stop light, town after town, had taken its' toll. We were tired and hungry. The usual restaurant on #74 had by now fed most late noon diners, so we had no delay in being seated. We ordered a light meal, so as not to slow the trip. Buck was not forgotten, I took him some water and a large hamburger.

After leaving Charlotte, the route along #74 was more open country; large stretches of farms and pine forest were a welcome relief from the towns that we had endured behind us. At four o'clock, the Barnes' house in Wilmington was an inviting sight!

Fred had come in early from the mill and he and Rachel welcomed us. After our bags were stowed inside, we were led to the large screened back porch. Rachel's maid served cool drinks, lemonade with crushed ice.

Talk centered around plans for the morrow. Betty and Rachel would go look at cars; Fred had arranged for the Marshall brothers up in Pender County to take us down the thoroughfare to the Black River, so George would be able to view the cypress and tupelo trees that I had bragged to him about.

That evening, we dined on the riverfront in downtown Wilmington; George was awe struck by the river traffic passing by; occasionally a ship or tugboat's horn would rattle the windows in the restaurant.

Saturday was to be a big day for all of us, especially Betty. Fred had not revealed to Rachel his business dealing with Betty and myself, therefore, she was under the impression that Betty could only afford to buy a used car. "Betty, dear, let's drive to the Chevrolet place, they sell used Cadillac's, I know you would love one; then there are other places that sell used cars." Rachel was insistent. Struggling to hold her tongue, Betty said they should take her car in case she wanted to trade it in, she had already consulted the yellow pages and knew exactly where she was going.

Driving to downtown, Betty stopped at Cameron & Cameron, dealers in BMW's. Parking in front of the display building, they got out. Rachel was shocked and asked why they were stopping here. "Oh, I just want to mosey" around," Betty laughed.

There were three new BMW's on display, one, a dark gray with red leather interior. As she approached the gray one, a smiling salesman greeted her and said "You must like this one." "Yes, it's nice, is it gas? I can't use diesel." "Yes, mam, it's gas," the man answered, "want to try it? I can have it ready in ten minutes." "I want to try it, can we drive it up #74 a ways to really open it up?" "Lady, we can drive it wherever you desire, wait in the lounge, it will be ready shortly," the salesman assured. While this was happening, Rachel stood by, awe struck, refusing to believe what she was hearing.

Shortly, the salesman appeared at the lounge and said the car was ready. Seated behind the wheel, Betty tried to fathom what the salesman was explaining, as he pointed out the various instruments and controls. Rachel seated in back, had to admit that even such luxury, as this was superior to her Cadillac. She had never driven Fred's BMW, or ridden in back. The controls work exactly like your little Ford, but you've got a lot more horses under the hood, so just take it slow and easy." The salesman advised.

Leaving Wilmington, the traffic thinned, and Betty became more confident and by the time they were on #74, she speeded up. Individual suspension on each wheel allowed a much smoother ride than an American made car. After a few minutes, Betty muttered, "I'm sold, let's go back and start the paperwork. I'll bring my husband in Monday and we can complete the purchase."

Fred drove his truck, although it was a bit crowded with we three in front; Buck rode in the back. Crawford and Haley Marshall were waiting for us at their boat landing on Lyons Canal. The canal would lead to the Thoroughfare and then into the Black River.

Two boats were necessary; Haley Marshall would handle one, with Fred and Buck riding with him, and George and I would go with Crawford. We were fortunate to be in the company of the Marshall brothers, for they had sold us hardwood veneer logs when I once worked in Wilmington. They knew every nook and cranny of the Cape Fear River lowlands.

Passage down Lyons Canal was slow, because the waterway was narrow and full of sunken logs. Cypress, tupelo and black gum trees lined the banks. George, intrigued with the huge cypress knees, Spanish moss and black water, studied the surroundings intently, as only an Indian could do. Crawford's booming voice above the soft put-put of the motor, kept us well supplied with his experiences from logging to hunting and fishing.

Of special interest to George, were the great, hollow cypress trees, which stood here and there, like guardian sentinels over the lower canopy below. Crawford explained that the reason they were still there was because of their defect; some were well over a thousand years old!

Presently, we entered the Thoroughfare; this was where part of the Cape Fear River divided and entered the Black River. Roan Island, to out right was formed as a result. Perhaps eons ago, the Thoroughfare was once the main part of the Cape Fear River! All things change, rivers, mountains, continents! What once was, is no more and then no more, changes into something new.

As we proceeded down the Thoroughfare, wood ducks took flight, and sliders (some call cocters) basking in the early sun, slid off logs; occasionally, a deer would be spotted, well ahead. Truly, the Cape Fear lowlands held a preponderance of life!

At the junction of the Thoroughfare and Black River, the Marshall's had erected a tarpaper hunting and fishing camp; here, we tied up. Crawford unloaded a large bag of groceries, along with a huge pot. "Now, you boys make yourselves comfortable, while Haley and me go down river and check out our fish traps. Did I spy part of a crank telephone slightly protruding from underneath a canvas in the boat?" Crawford, with a sheepish grin towards me, jumped on the boat and cranked the motor.

While the brothers were "checking fish traps", we busied ourselves with gathering dry wood lying around or lodged against trees during spring's freshets. Occasionally, the chug, chug of the diesel powered tug boats could be heard, as they traveled up and down the Cape Fear River, three or four miles to the west.

Presently, we could hear the sound of an outboard motor, coming from down river and less than two minutes later, Crawford tied his boat to the shore. The fisherman had filled a bushel basket with both channel cats and flat heads!

While we made a fire, Crawford and Haley skinned the catfish, it was amazing how fast the brothers could rip the skin from a catfish, using a knife and pliers! After skinned, the fish were filleted and cut into two-inch chunks. Washing the chunks, Crawford placed then into a large pot with water; this was brought to a boil and left for five minutes, until the meat was tender. The water was then poured off.

The meat was taken out, then, layers of it re-introduced to cover the bottom of the pot. Next, a layer of thick-sliced tomatoes covered the fish, followed by a layer of scalloped potatoes. The process was the repeated until it filled the pot to its' halfway point. Also added to each layer was a sprinkling of salt, black and cayenne pepper. I suspect that Crawford had also introduced a leaf or so of bay leaves, although he was very secretive with his formula! A half of cup of finely chopped onions were added to each layer of potatoes. After forty-five minutes, the heat was reduced to only a simmer; then three quarts of whole milk was gently stirred in, making sure the milk did not boil (boiled milk will curdle). The stew was allowed to simmer for perhaps ten to fifteen minutes, then, Crawford ladled the steaming contents out to us in paper bowls. Was this delicious? It was out of this world!

After we had gone back for seconds and could hold no more, Crawford suggested that we take the route back to the landing, by way of going around Roan Island and up to the Cape Fear River. Here, we had an opportunity to view large strands of virgin tupelo gum forests, intermixed with cypress. Although, I was very familiar with such scenes as these, it was a much exhilarating experience for George.

That evening beck in Wilmington, Rachel kept raving about Betty buying the BMW. "I just couldn't get over it." She kept saying.

The next morning, we drove down to the dealership and completed the purchase; George would drive the Ford and I would take the Jeep. Now, Betty could lead our caravan with her BMW!

We spent the afternoon at Wrightsville Beach, George had never been in the ocean before and delighted in romping in the water. That evening, we dined at Faircloth's, with its' usual excellent seafood.

Although we hated to leave such delightful surroundings and over the protests of Rachel and Fred, urgent business beckoning from

Jackson County, demanded that we must leave. Betty, leading the way in her new BMW, headed us westward.

After Keeper had filled his stomach with a juicy groundhog, he tested the currents and moved up the mountain; his destination, the great pass. Warm weather quarters, of course, were the large boulders in the pass. The big snake moved rapidly, constantly checking the currents, ever on the alert for enemies. By noon, he had reached the boulders, but a change in the weather had ushered in a front from the north. The front had overpowered the normal air currents generally drifting up the pass, and now Keeper detected fumes from the chain saws, of Frank's crews, cutting the right of way on the other side. This was disturbing, even upsetting; Keeper had to continue his journey, he must find out the source of the fumes.

The snake moved up the pass in rapid order and when the top was reached, the stato blast of trees cracking and crashing, combined with men yelling and four saws running, was over whelming. Keeper was angry, his once peaceful domain was now being violated. Well, there was nothing he could do about it but be would exact his measure later. He turned and went back to the boulders.

If we were ever to move out of the store in Cashiers, the Norton house would have to virtually be rebuilt, that is, wiring, plumbing and three bathrooms installed. The house was rather large, with five bedrooms upstairs and three on the first floor. After the basic wiring and plumbing were completed, then oil furnace system had to be installed. The roof was metal and sound, but needed repainted. Walls would be paneled and floors refinished. The plain facts were that I simply had more important things facing me and it would be up to Betty and George to get the Norton house completed. Betty would direct what she wanted done and George would engage the contractors to do the actual work. Now that we had a thorough plan in place for the house, I could spend full time to develop the mine.

According to the Asheville Citizen Times, a new ski resort was being erected near Boone; the article went on to state that a Denver, Colorado company was presently surveying the site and had already established a field office there.

I placed a call to Information, Boone and they gave me the field office number. When I called, the number, the person on the other end rather gruffly said they were not hiring at present. When I explained my purpose in calling, his tone instantly became more friendly, even apologetic. We agreed that I would meet with their chief engineer at two o'clock on the morrow. After a brief pause, Betty agreed that I could drive her new BMW, if she could accompany me; "I've always wanted to see Boone." She said.

It was a long, winding way from Cashiers to Boone and we left at seven o'clock next morning. Buck had to go with us, as it was too short of notice to leave him with George.

When we reached Asheville, we took #70 to Morganton, then #64 to Lenoir. From Lenoir, #321 led us to Boone. Our destination was actually located at Blowing Rock, only seven miles from Boone. Since we had plenty of time and Betty wanted to see Boone, we stopped there first for a hasty lunch.

Boone, the county seat of Watauga County, is also home of Appalachian State University. Boone is a beautiful town, nestled in the heart of surrounding mountains and even in mid summer, the nights are chilly due to its' high elevation. To the west of Boone, high mountains rise to over five thousand feet. Daniel Boone built a cabin in Boone and from here, he launched hunting trips to the surrounding mountains and in to Kentucky[3].

Rockford Construction Company from Denver, Colorado was the prime contractor for the ski resort, their field office, located just a stone's throw to the west of Blowing Rock wasn't too difficult to find, especially after we stopped and inquired about it! The office itself was nothing more than an extra large mobile motor home.

At our knock, we were invited in and greeted warmly by a rather large man, who introduced himself as the chief engineer. Following his introduction, he asked if we had eaten lunch. We thanked him, as we looked around; the office portion was crammed with maps; maps of all kinds, such as topographic and engineering surveys. Two other men were pouring over a large aerial photograph, apparently trying to reconcile it with a topographic map.

The chief engineer then got down to business, "Mr. Butler, I understand from our telephone conversation, that you want to construct an overhead tramway system." "Yes, since a road would be extremely difficult to build, I thought that an overhead cableway would be the

3   Daniel Boone by John Preston Arthur, Chapter IV, 1914.

fastest and most practical system to put in; this would only extend to twelve hundred feet and support a weight of two tons. I need this system put in as soon as possible." I tried to sound as urgent as possible, without conveying a tone of desperation. "Mr. Butler, on the surface, what you apparently need, would not be difficult to build, however, I have a schedule to meet here; we have to complete this system by the first of December, next year. Now, we own part interest in a company in Klamath, Oregon. This company is well experienced, since they manufacture and erect overhead cable systems for the logging industry out there. I can have their engineer to come out and meet with you in two days." After taking down all the pertinent information that I could give him, we thanked the engineer and left for Cashiers.

Although any construction company that would eventually put in our overhead cable system could produce their electricity with a portable generator, I needed to get started on a permanent electrical system that would supply the mine. From the Holden house, the new line would entail about eight miles of new line. After the Boone trip I drove to Sylva and found a branch office of Hiwassee Power Company. The manager said that if the right of way was already cleared, the eight miles of line, would cost around nine thousand dollars; I told him to get started as soon as possible after I paid half of the cost. Since he was familiar with the Holden place, he assured me that they could start in two weeks.

In two days, I met a representative of the Klamath Machinery Company at the Jackson County Court House; the man had flown in to the Asheville airport (located just south of the city) and rented a car and drove to Sylva. It was after four in the afternoon, too late to visit the mine site, but we drove to Glenville, where the man would spend the night with the Holden's.

Next morning, I drove the Jeep to Glenville and picked up Frank and the Klamath man. The late September day was cool, but the temperature would rapidly climb; this could possibly invite a late fall storm, so I wasted no time in reaching the end of the mountain road.

Here, we parked and started walking, or I should say, crawling and scrambling over the logs that Frank's crew left where the right of way was cut. It took almost an hour to reach the mine site; here, we sat down and rested and had a chance to discuss the situation.

Concerned that the terrain might be too severe to put a system in,

I broached the subject. The Klamath man laughed; "You should see some of the country where they were logging; some of the slopes are seventy degrees; this area would be no problem for us." I felt relieved. "I will have to bring in a couple of men and spend some time here to make a profound study before I can give you a proposal; that will take a few days. Let's see, the steel can come in by rail to Sylva; it would have to be trucked to the landing here; is there a trucker in Sylva?" Frank had been following the conversation, spoke, "No problem, I can truck the steel and other equipment to the landing here." "Well, that's good to know, it will make things more simple for me," the Klamath engineer agreed, "also Mr. Holden, I may need you to run some of your equipment, such as a small bulldozer." "Yes, I agreed with Mr. Butler that I would help with the construction, if I was needed," Frank nodded.

I continued to ask questions. "Where do you plan to stay while the construction is going on?" "We bring a large motor home and park it on site; it's self contained and will accommodate seven people, including the cook. I noticed below a nice creek; we can keep our reservoir filled from it." "Well then, I asked, how will you be able to move equipment and materials over this rough terrain with logs and boulders all over the place?" "That is simple, the engineer answered, after we first set up living quarters, then we put an overhead line with a rehaul system; with this thing, we can move materials in the air all along the right of way. It is just like an overhead logging rig." "Well, it sounds like you know exactly how to approach this thing," I marveled. "Thank you sir, yes, I can say that we are well experienced; now, I'll return in a few days with some more men and make a study, then hopefully give you a figure and we can sign a contract. You say that winter will probably set in by mid-November, if things go well, maybe we can get some work accomplished by then; over all though, it should take no more than two months to complete the job. The balance of the work would have to continue next spring."

The most important job connected to the processing of the gems was a strong secure building. This would be where the chunks of matrix rocks were brought in off the mountain, broken up, and the crystals extracted. First, I considered locating the building near the Holden place, but on further reflections, the thought occurred that this might expose the family to some kind of danger; the idea was discarded. A building on my land, near the entrance to the mountain road would probably be a better location. It would be more isolated and have to be guarded when in operation. First, before getting started on the building, however, there was something else that I wanted to accomplish.

All of us were thrilled in camping at the Overhang campsite. The problem was carrying all the food and gear up the mountain; it was just an excruciating affair. Why not have a trail pushed out with a bulldozer, where a small four-wheel drive vehicle could negotiate? Hunters used such machines to access the most difficult terrain. A system such as this would make our camping trips to the Overhang much more pleasant!

I drove by the Holden place and found the men doing maintenance work on their equipment. Frank agreed to put Tommy on the job with a small D-4 bulldozer as soon as I could lay out the trail. Generally, the trail would wind around any trees and boulders, but when the steep terrain near the top was approached, some excavating and leveling would be necessary.

While Betty and George were continuing to supervise the restoration work on the Norton house, so much work had, by now, been accomplished, that the building had taken on and amazing transformation. For instance, the entire south wall in the kitchen had been replaced by a large picture window. Now, we could eat in the kitchen while enjoying the view below in the valley and the mountains beyond! To get all this work done though, it seemed that the two supervisors had hired every contractor in Jackson County! I left them to continue their devices and now I had to start flagging the trail. Walking outside, there was Buck lying in the shade, snoozing away. "Get up, you overweight rascal and come with me." He eyed me reluctantly yawned, got to his feet and tagged along.

We started about a quarter of a mile towards the bridge. With a hand compass that had vertical degrees, I followed an upward course westward, trying to stay on a five - degree angle. Hopefully, this would lead to the top of the orchard. Every few yards, a tree would be flagged, fore and aft. Each hundred yards or so, I would line the last flagged tree behind me with the farthest sightable flag behind that one; this way, the correct course could be maintained. Of course, the bulldozer operator would try to follow the flags as he moved on either side of the marked trees.

When we came in sight of the orchard, I could see that the trail would lead to the foot of the long, white oak ridge, just above the orchard. Not bad, I thought, starting from a known point and ending up just a few yards off your unseen target! We continued on the same course, crossing the ridge and ascending ever upward. Finally, I reversed directions, which would lead to the Overhang.

The terrain was growing ever steeper and many times, the five degree slope had to be exceeded. It was obvious now that I would have to come back tomorrow to complete the job. When we reached the Norton house, Tommy Norton was there unloading his bulldozer. I drove him down to the starting point on the road and he would begin work in the morning.

Now that work on the Norton house was nearing completion, it was Betty's lot to get the place furnished. Up to now, it had only the bare essentials, two beds, a wood kitchen range, kitchen table and icebox. The array necessary to furnish this house was like trying to outfit a small hotel. Betty would spend two days in Asheville, selecting the furnishings. She wanted an all-electric kitchen, but along with an electric stove, we would absolutely keep the wonderful wood range. Nothing beats a meal cooked on a wood stove! Well, all this was up to Betty; I had other things to do. George was after the contractors to build a large equipment shed to house several vehicles.

The following day, I kept on flagging the trail and finished just in time to get back home before dark. Tommy was well into pushing the trail, but would be lucky to finish before winter set in.

A week after we had met with the Klamath engineer, he had met with two men, and they were now marking a survey for the cable system. I hoped to get a proposal from them in another week, for October was just a week away.

One of the contractors that had been working on the Norton house was a commercial builder from Sylva. While he was still doing some work on the equipment shed, I had a chance to sit down and go over some preliminary plans that I had drawn up for the gem processing building. The plan called for a fifty by fifty foot building that was made entirely of reinforced concrete. The front section would be for processing and the rear for storage, including a vault. An adjoining small building would house a compressor and auxiliary generator, although the building would be wired. The contractor agreed to modify my plan up grade the engineering standards and submit a proposal.

By the tenth of October, the hardwoods were now flaunting their colors in full, reminding me of an over flowering Gypsy dancer in the breezes. It had frosted too, in the bottoms and ice had formed on the mountaintops. Now, it was time for Keeper to abandon his warm weather habitat in the great pass and search for food in the lower elevations. Not liked to be rushed, this would give him plenty of time to fulfill the search.

A beehive of activity, stretching from the mine site to the bottom of the mountain, reverberated back and forth. Three contractors, pushing their crews to the limit, were trying to accomplish some work before winter would call a halt. Hiwassee Power Company had set the poles in place and were now stretching some eight miles of line, from Holden place to the truck landing near the mine location.

Klamath Engineering was pouring footings for hanger supports; the concrete would have to be allowed to set for fifteen days. By that time however, November might usher in a snow and the men, well aware of this, hastened their work.

The building contractor from Sylva was pouring concrete for the processing building, which was located at the bottom of the mountain road. Most likely, they could work much longer here than the two people high up the mountain.

Keeper moved down the pass, all the while carefully testing the currents. His chief concern was an encounter with a young, inexperienced bear; one that didn't mind starting a ruckus, but would not understand what the dire consequences might be. Then too, a mother bear with cubs would also be dangerous.

At the bottom of the pass, he turned westward and followed the trail, leading toward the Overhang, and reaching the Camp, he rested for a long spell. There had been no recent human presence detected, so he relaxed in contentment.

Following the respite, the big snake left the Overhang and turned down the mountain, headed toward the white oak ridge, his favorite hunting ground.

Keeper did not have to descend very far, until loud noises coming from below told him something was wrong; his forked tongue also picked up the scent of exhaust fumes. This warned him that humans were ahead and now, all creatures shun this place. Pausing in confusion, he rested here for a long time. There was another hunting ground that he had used many years ago, but it was a long ways away; it was on the Galloway lands. Urged by the cool fall weather, he turned and headed eastwards.

Crossing the creek below the pass, he pressed onward, until the Galloway lands were reached.

Hunting wild hogs was dangerous, at least for a snake. To begin with, they could not be approached out in the open, for he could get himself surrounded from all sides. They would have to be ambushed from a safe place, somewhere along their trail, that an over hanging rock was located to the feeding grounds.

By now, it was growing late in the afternoon. So Keeper must find temporary sleeping quarters for the coming night; he did not relish spending the night out in the open.

Moving on, he suddenly came to a well-used hog trail; it wound through the middle and downward of a hardwood ridge. This indicated to Keeper, that the hogs might be denning somewhere below. Descending along the trail, he suddenly came to a large hollow tress that had fallen and broken in half. The trail had simply led between the two halves and the hollow logs were an ideal ambush spot. Choosing the hollow closest to the trail, Keeper crawled in for the night!

For three days, Keeper watched and waited expectantly; then early in the morning on the fourth day, his fortune changed. Below, an explosion of sound jolted him awake and it was coming nearer by the seconds. Fully awake now and alert, he poked his immense head toward the opening in the log; his senses warned him of heavy vibrations and odors. Suddenly a young bear appeared, huffing and bawling at every lunge, he was being followed by a huge, angry sow hog, chumping her jaws, with tushs clicking like the sound of many castanets. Following her was her brood of young pigs.

As the bear and sow whizzed by the log, all her brood jammed up at the narrow opening between the two logs. This gave Keeper the opportunity that he had for so long been waiting for. Without a moment's hesitation, he selected one of the larger piglets and struck, snatching it inside the logs. As the whole entourage swept on up the mountain, Keeper began to relish his long awaited meal. Tomorrow, he would go back to the cave, near the Overhang, his winter quarters. Here, on warm days, he would crawl out and sun himself on a nearby ledge. As it became colder, he would take up residence in the cave.

Towards the last of October, Tommy had pushed the trail to the upper end of the long, white oak ridge. Up to now, the pushing had been relatively level, for the mountain slope, rarely exceeded twenty degrees. Now, the mountain slope abruptly changed from twenty degrees to forty-five degrees. This meant that vast amounts of dirt would have to be removed in order to get a fairly level bed. A larger tractor was needed, so Holden brought in a D-6 Caterpillar and a second operator. While the larger tractor pushed ahead, the smaller one could level the roadbed. There was yet another mile to reach the Overhang and they would be lucky to finish before a deep snow would intervene.

In the meantime, I ordered a new golf cart through the golf club at Asheville. This thing had a low ground clearance and now Frank Holden was reworking it to suit mountain conditions. With larger wheels it would ride over obstacles in the trail. A four by six foot bed in the rear, allowed for holding food and camping gear.

Beautiful dry weather continued all through October and even into the middle of November. All the hanger supports were now in place and the Klamath contractors had erected the first hanger, when the weather turned sour. Warnings were broadcast, well in advance, and when the "Siberian Express" hit the area, it hit with a vengeance. The contractor had to abandon the cableway job until the following spring.

Holden had reached the Overhang, but by now, the trail was useless, a deep snow had taken care of that. Construction had simply come to an abrupt halt. George and I had missed our beloved hunting due to all the on going activity, now, we had to make the best of coming winter.

Even though the Norton house was now livable to out standards, Betty and I chose to winter over in Cashiers. The store was comfortable, conveniently located and our friends were near. During Christmas, we spent a delightful week with the Barnes' in Wilmington. Fred had made plans for us to enter the spring auction in New York, during early June. That, of course, would all depend on how soon we could get the mine in operation.

After Christmas, the weather began to turn mild, at least enough, so that the contractor could resume work on the processing building. Since the basic structure had been completed during late fall, now the plumbing and wiring were being installed. Also, for added security, a high chain linked fence, topped with razor wire, was being built around the building.

Although snow lingered on the higher peaks, the elevation at the mine site allowed the Klamath people to resume work on the tramway and by May 15th, the work was completed. The power company had extended the line from the truck landing, out to the mine site.

Everything was now completed, except the small utility building next to the mine. Although the buildings framework was metal, the floor and sides had to be heavy oak planking. Since wood is a good insulator, the building would offer protection to the mine crew if a sudden thunderstorm might occur.

Did we need water to cool the air-hydraulic drills and cement breaker tools, which would be used? Frank strongly suggested that we would. Where was the water though; only a trickle dripped from the rocks above? Down below, some six hundred feet was plenty of water; it was where we had scooped up on Betty's garnets. How could sand and cement or lumber for the frame be transported to this location? It was simply almost impossible. Frank Holden came up with the idea that we could bring in two large metal watering troughs over the tram, and easily pull them down to the small waterfall; this we did! A long, flexible hose connected the receptacles to a pump above and we had water!

A heavy compressor and tools were brought in over the tram and stored in the small utility building. Now, we were really ready to start mining.

A mining permit was needed before we could formally start operations. I called the North Carolina Department of Natural Resources and they said for me to write a report on what we would be doing, then, after studying the report, they would send some engineers and inspectors up to make their own evaluations.

In my report, I stated that no blasting would be used because this would most likely shatter the crystals and the mining process would be done with air-hydraulic equipment. A week transpired after sending in my report; the, they called and said they were sending their people up to study the situations. When the group arrived, they spent a full day on the mountain. I made it a point to have Frank Holden present and they seemed impressed that he had in the past worked for a feldspar mine. After a week's time, I had to go to Raleigh to sign documents and receive the permits. Now we were ready to mine. There was one important thing left and that was to employ some guards. Frank and his crew simply could not work during the day and guard the mine at night.

I discussed the guard situation with George; he was silent for several minutes before speaking then, "I think I might know what we can do; tomorrow, let's drive over to Cherokee. I'll call some people tonight."

George stopped by the store next morning; he preferred that we go in his pick-up truck. Buck was whining to go with us, so I told him to jump in the back. An hour and half later, George pulled up at the police station in Cherokee; mow, I reasoned, he is going to talk to his nephews and sure enough, they were waiting for us in the lounge.

Both Henry and Phillip had been marine snipers, serving in the South Pacific during WWII. Now, they were with the Cherokee Council Police. After the usual "small talk", we got down to business.

George had already told me all about their salaries and benefits, so based on this knowledge, I knew about what to offer them. Their salaries were fifty dollars a week, with uniforms and vehicles and other expenses provided. Also, they had medical and life insurance. When we broached the subject, they at first seemed to be somewhat shocked. After all, they loved their jobs and were intensely loyal to the Council.

I began by saying that we were opening a mining operation and it would have to be guarded by experienced people who were honest and loyal. I also told them that I knew that they had the qualifications for the job. "Now, I am prepared to offer you a permanent position, with double your present pay, a vehicle and other pertinent equipment and living quarters on the premise. You will be insured both health and life. At the end of each year, if the company has made a profit, ten percent of that profit will be divided among all employees, and incidentally, we will not employ more than ten people. I need an answer from you as soon as possible, for we will be opening the mine in a weeks' time." I know the brothers would have to think about this for some time; for after all, it had suddenly been sprung on them. We left, by saying that they could keep in touch with George, when their decision was made.

I had a mobile home placed near the processing building. From here it was a simple matter to hook up the water and the electricity for the facility.

Without fanfare or any kind of publicity, we started operations at the mine on Monday, of the second week in May. The Owl brothers had accepted my offer and they had moved their possessions into the mobile home.

The method of extracting chunks of crystal bearing rocks from their source, was to drill two inch diameter holes, some ten to twelve inches deep, then a cone shaped round wedge was started in the holes, hence, a modified air hammer pounded the wedge until a chink of rock was broken off its' source. Frank Holden and his twin sons would work the mine two days and produce enough chunks to keep the crew in the processing building busy for at least a week or more.

In the processing building, we used small hand-held air tools to gouge out the crystals. Once a crystal was exposed, extreme care had to be taken so as not to damage the gem. It became obvious from the very beginning, that all of us would have to build up considerable experience before avoiding any damage to the crystals. We worked the mine and processing plant only when on a special order. The workday was six hours, and the number of days worked depended on the size of the work order.

Pangs of hunger had roused Keeper from his winter sleep; it had been around the twentieth of April and too cool to hang around the cave. At this altitude, there was still little evidence of spring greenery. Down below, however, leaves were popping out and the daytime temperature was inviting the usual dinner guests to the orchard. Fall apple crop had been prodigious and now there were numerous frozen apples left under the leaves.

Once he had emerged from the cave, the big snake headed straight down the mountain; he wanted no part of this chilly atmosphere outside the cave. His senses ever on the alert for danger or food, he proceeded rapidly toward the orchard. On pervious excursions, Keeper had found a temporary shelter under a ledge, which was right next to a game trail. He had even taken a small pig here. From here then, it was only a stone's throw to the orchard. Keeper would spend all of May down here and as warm weather crept up the mountain, he would go to his summer haunt in the great pass.

CHAPTER VII

Face to Face

Fred called from Wilmington, concerned whether we would be ready for the summer auction in New York. It was an international affair, held twice a year, in early summer and late fall. Buyers and sellers from the world over came to purchase or sell, unpolished, precious stones. From Amsterdam and South Africa with diamonds, Burma with sapphires and rubies, Columbia with emeralds; yes, from the world over, they flocked to the three-day event.

Working a six hour shift, five days a week, we had started operations in mid-May, when Fred called. I assured him that we would have emeralds available, but at the moment, I couldn't put a number on how many stones, or the total weight of karats, there would be. The stones were sold in batches, not as singles. The batches had to be weighed and total karats labeled on each box of stones, and also, the crystals had to be certified as to the authenticity. The qualification had to be done by a certified jeweler and in my case, the Finkelstein Brothers would be the ones. Henry and Phillip Owl, nephews of George Owl, had attended the Marine Armament School, Quantico, Virginia, at my insistence. Even though the two had served in WWII as Marine snipers, I felt that too much time had elapsed since leaving active duty; then too, serving as just police officers did not expose them to the dangers that they could face, guarding the mine and also, the processing building. When they had finished the sixty-day refresher course, I had equipped them with the finest sniper rifles available, Remington Model 700 special target rifles, with Nikon telescopic sights. Despite being unwieldy to carry around, this gun, firing the 300 H&H Magnum bullet, was capable of centering a 10 inch target at one thousand yards. For side arms, they carried 9mm Browning auto loading pistols. They also carried 9mm Schmeisser machine guns, which were considered to be the best guns of it's type in WWII. George Owl, Frank Holden and myself, also carried the Schmeisser. These were fully automatic and required a Federal Fire Arms permit.

Surrounding the processing building was a high chain link fence and I had bought two German Shepherd dogs that roamed inside the fence. Both Owl brothers had to become thoroughly acquainted with the dogs so that they could handle them when on patrol. Now, I felt that I had done my best to secure the mine and the processing building.

As Tommy Holden pushed the trail to the Overhang, I wanted to extend it from here, eastward to the creek and at the beginning to the pass. This was easier going because the ground formed a wide bench and therefore relatively level. I intended to keep Tommy busy pushing roads and trails over much of the property, including the huge Calloway tract. The reason for this was simple, if a forest fire occurred, we could reach it more easily. When property is managed for timber production, game management and recreational activity access to all parts is essential.

The small landing strip near Sylva consisted with nothing more than a modest building, equipped with a telephone and other essential equipment. Also, a fuel tank and minor repair service was available. The owner had several four place aircraft. This was fortunate for the citizens of Jackson County, for in case of a dire emergency, a patient could be flown to the Duke Hospital or any other facility. The manager of the airport was also not averse to making a fast dollar "under the table" if that situation should present itself!

On June the first, Mario Pascano, Lieutenant in the new York Mafia, received a telephone call from the small Sylva airport, "The Butlers have opened the mine here:, it said. The caller was told to stand by for further instructions.

Pascano immediately went to his boss, Frank Carlucci, Director of the New York Mafia with the information. "I want you to call the man and have him pick you up at the Asheville – Fletcher airport in his plane, then fly over the whole area around the mine and get me some good aerial photographs. Also, get some up-to-date county road maps. I want to pin point the exact location of the mine." Lieutenant Pascano was delighted with the assignment, now, he was in his natural element – running down special projects!

Early June weather became unusually warm, in fact, down right uncomfortable for Keeper to remain near the cave. What was he to do? That monstrous noise making machine, spitting out its' foul smelling smoke, and jarring the atmosphere around, he just had to leave the cave. He wanted to go to the boulders, in the cool pass, but the machine was between him and the trail, so he headed below the path, and hurrying to get well in front of the machine, he proceeded toward the creek and then turned upward. At last the boulders were reached; perhaps the machine would not follow him in the pass. If Tommy Holden had been aware of the snakes' predicament, he would have shut the machine off and allowed the snake to pass by, since I had instructed that no form of wildlife was to be disturbed. When the noisy machine would leave the immediate are, Keeper would divide his time between the boulders and the cave.

On Sunday, June 6, a small plane spent an hour over the mine and made wide sweeps from the Holden house, clear across the mountain to the Norton place. From the Norton house, it swung over to Highway #107 and followed the road towards Sylva. The Owl brothers, who had spent most of Saturday night and up into the wee hours of Sunday morning, patrolling the mine and processing building, were asleep when the plane came over, so they were not aware of its' presence.

By the 10th of June, I was satisfied that we now had more than enough crystals to compete with the Columbian Consortium, the count was 300, but Finklestein Brothers would have to place a Karat figure on them. They were crated, sealed and Wells-Fargo transported the lot to Finklestein. After certification, they would remain there until the day before the auction, where they would be placed in the hands of Auctioneers International, Ltd.

The auction had been kicked back to Monday, June 21st, it ran the 21st through the 23rd and ended in a giant banquet on Wednesday night. Betty, George and I would attend from Jackson County with Fred and Rachel Barnes from Wilmington. Thursday evening, I left Buck with the Holdens; by now, he was well acquainted with the family, so we were confident that he would be fine.

We left Cashiers on Friday, Betty drove the BMW, now, I could sit back and enjoy the scenery, or the landscapes swept by. George settled comfortably in back, occasionally snoozed. At noon, we stopped in Charlotte for a bite to eat; our favorite restaurant located along side of east #74, specialized in barbeque. It is often said that the further south you go, the barbeque gets better. I have tasted none better than that made in the "Ol' North State".

Fred had left the sawmill early; he and Rachel were waiting in the yard, as we drove up. This trip was to be strictly business, so the Barnes had not planned any extravagant affair for us. We all wanted to be well rested, fresh for the coming event. Fred had made reservations for the five people at the Waldorf Astoria. The auction would run from 10 am on Monday until 3 pm on Wednesday. Wednesday evening was to be a gala affair, put on by Auctioneers International. One could speculate as to how much this would cost the company!

Friday evening, the dinner down by the riverfront in Wilmington as a delight: river traffic up and down the Cape Fear lent excitement, as only such as atmosphere could produce.

Saturday was devoted to Wrightsville Beach, at the Barnes' waterfront house. All of us, fortified with light "adult beverages" capered about in the surf. The usual dinner at Faircloth's over, we left to go back to Wilmington. Our Piedmont flight would leave at one pm, Sunday afternoon, putting un in New York at three.

Piedmont had vastly upgraded their Wilmington planes; originally they had purchased a fleet of wartime C-47s and converted them to civilian use. The civilian model was known as the DC-6. Now, with more power and with luxury interior furbishing, they represented state of the art, for small, twin engine, commercial aeroplanes.

I should mention our seating arrangement, for they turned out to be both significant and hilarious. While Betty and I sat across the isle from Rachel and Fred, George sat in front of us, and who occupied the seat next to him? No other than an overweight lady, wearing a flowery, wide brimmed hat. The flight had only been underway just a few minutes, when the lady introduced herself and struck up a conversation, which continued on for two hours – poor George! If the poor man got a word in edgewise, we were not aware of it! Occupying the sear in back of Fred and Rachel was Lieutenant Mario Pascano, well within earshot of any conversation that might interest him. When the flight ended, we thought we were leaving the hot, sultry weather in Wilmington, but were disappointed to find that New York was just as bad! Evidently, the vast concrete and brick buildings that made up New York, absorbed more heat than smaller cities, elsewhere. Two cabs whisked us to Park Avenue in midtown, Manhattan and there it was – the Waldorf Astoria! This American icon is home to many famous people, the world over. Here all kinds of national and international events are held.

Fred had not scheduled any social events for our group; there would be plenty of time for this after the auction was finished. Tomorrow, we wanted to be well rested and fresh. Sunday evening, after a light dinner at the hotel, we retired early.

Auctioneers International, Ltd., located on 5th Avenue, was headquartered in a large building and could easily accommodate five hundred registered guests, plus an array of security people.

Since our group were participants and pre-registered, we were checked and issued numbers, just in case we wanted to submit a bid. Rear half of the large auction room was seating capacity for quests; the front half was filled with glass enclosed tables, holding the day's stones to be auctioned. Each table was labeled after the name of the seller, his origin and the type of jewels displayed. Buyers and sellers could freely circulate among the many tables and study the glass-protected contents. Armed guards also circulated freely among the people and many were concentrated near the tables.

Tables were grouped according to the stones it held and ours was next to the large Columbian Consortium. Our stones were much larger than the Columbian and more people crowded around. From ten o'clock until eleven, prospective buyers and sellers kept circulating and minutely studying the tables of their interest and promptly at eleven, the gong sounded. "Ladies and Gentlemen, you have exactly ten minutes to be seated, then the auction will begin."

To our consternation, the auction began at the diamond tables and there were several of them. It was anyone's guess as to how long activity here would continue. Also, there were other tables of rubies and sapphires between us and the diamond tables.

Amsterdam was considered one of the worlds' top diamond

processing centers. Here, what is known as the Lasard method of cutting and polishing diamonds is employed. Now Americans had become more involved in diamond processing, so there was much activity around the diamond tables until the auction ended at three pm.

It was not until day three that the auctioneers finally got to our table. The Columbian section ended at the close of day two. Our auction began at eleven, when everyone was fresh. Due to the size of our stones and also being the first North American Company of any size to produce emeralds, all our emeralds were sold.

One such buyer was Romero, Ltd., they had bid on a 2,000 Karat lot, which brought $200,000. Later, we were to learn that Romero, Ltd. was not only a large jewelry company, but a front for the New York Mafia.

Two hours after the auction began, all our stones were sold; I won't mention the price that they bought, except it was in the millions. Naturally, all of us were, more or less, in a state of shock, which later turned to jubilation, as the fact sank in. The end results were probably similar to betting on the winning horse at the Kentucky Derby.

Auctioneers International, Ltd. not only moved gems from seller to buyer, they entertained lavishly at the end of each major event. Their ballroom was large enough to accommodate some five hundred guests. After all, the company could afford to put on such an extravaganza, for they received a ten percent commission on all the transactions.

Some forty or more circular tables bedecked with linen, crystal and silverware, occupied most of the room, with each table seating twelve guests. Buyers and sellers were grouped together. Each guest had a golden engraved identification card placed at his place. Betty sat to my left and Mr. Frank Carlucci of Romero, Inc. was next on my right. George Owl, Fred and Rachel Barnes sat across the table. Other guests there were buyers from Amsterdam.

Promptly at eight, the banquet began with a welcome from Auctioneers, then followed a twelve piece band. As drinks softened the atmosphere around, we began to introduce ourselves.

Mr. Carlucci, to my right, thrust a large diamond studded hand towards me and smiling, introduced himself, "I'm Frank Carlucci, of Romero, Inc.; I'm certainly pleased with the quality of your gems." "Thank you, sir. I'm Robert Butler, and I'm proud to produce such stones." To Betty's left were the Amsterdam buyers, and we were introduced to them. They expressed the pleasure of a second source of emeralds; now, the Columbian consortium would have some competition to deal with and perhaps Amsterdam could fill their orders with more reasonable prices!

As the evening wore on, Carlucci became more vocal and began to tell me about his worldwide connections in marketing jewelry. "We have connections in Europe and Asia, most especially in India. The people there must worship jewelry as much as their sacred cows," he laughed.

"Mr. Butler, I would be very much interested in buying into your company, say a twenty-five percent interest. My company could open up direct sales worldwide and you would not have to depend on an auction. Think of what an advantage this would be. Let's say, I could offer you twenty million dollars, for a twenty-five percent interest in your company." "Well, Mr. Carlucci, that seems like a mighty generous offer, but at this time, I plan to keep my company within the family. I can make my own decisions and not have to be beholden to other people." At this, I could sense that Carlucci was not pleased, especially, when he coldly stated that he hoped I would not regret his offer.

As the evening wore on, we met more of the Amsterdam people and they, too, expressed the desire to deal directly with our company without having to go through an auction. This suited me fine since the auction company took a portion of the proceeds as a commission and also Finklestein & Finklestein charged for grading and certifying the stones to prepare them for the auction. Well, this was now Fred's department; it was up to him to follow up these contacts. After the meal, we were able to meet other buyers, especially the Indians from Bombay and Calcutta; they were very prominent in jewelry manufacturing. The gala ended at eleven o'clock and were we ever tired!

We slept late next morning and met our flight back to Wilmington at one o'clock. Early June and the water at Wrightsville Beach was too cold to enter, but we spent two days there with the Barnes, just walking on the beach or lounging on the front porch. Early evenings, we dined at several restaurants; in fact, so much so, that I got tired of eating out and longed for Betty's home cooking!

Fred's commission from the auction brought him over a million dollars and this was as much as his sawmill would have made in five years. Fred had made many contacts during the auction , and now that we had grown substantially as a result, he would have to spend full time traveling. Worried about the sawmill, he consulted me, "Bob, I simply don't have the time for the mill and do the job that you require of me, what should I do?" "Well, Fred it should be obvious, either sell the mill or get someone to run it full time; that is of course if you want to stay on with us, because, I plan to run the mine and won't have time to be involved with merchandising the stones. I would hope that you would go full time with us." "For sure, I want to stay with you, so I'll talk to my mill superintendent; I know that he can run the mill, but he won't have time to supply the mill with logs." "Well, then, your problem seems to be procuring a timber man for the mill; you need an experienced man for this. We have three months until the mine is started up again for the late fall auction, in the meantime, maybe you can hire a procurement man." "Well, Bob, I'll try, and if I can't fine a person for this, I'll just close the mill down, because I certainly plan to stay with you." Fred was empathetic on this issue.

Once again back in Cashiers, we now had some three months before operating the mine for the fall event. Frank and his twin sons could go back to raising cattle and running heavy equipment, but I wanted Tommy to spend full time building roads on the mountain. Henry and Phillip Owl would guard the mine. Of course, Betty would continue to finish the Norton house.

My job was to flag the right of way for the numerous roads that Tommy and his helper would be working on.

George and I promised each other that when we had the time, we would try to open an entrance to the cave. I had purchased a portable air compressor and a small pavement breaker. This equipment would be much easier and faster to use, than using a sledgehammer and chisels. Too, now that we could transport some light equipment up the mountain in my golf cart, we would not be dead tired by the time the job was reached!

The giant plate, that eons ago had slid down the mountain above and covered the entrance to the cave was at least four or five feet thick, and it was hard granite! It would not be easy to punch an opening to the cave, even with power tools!

Frank Carlucci, head of the New York mafia, leaning back in the plush leather chair, his feet on the desk, stared at the blue smoke, curling, lazily upward. Presently, he tapped the end of the Havana on the ash tray and inhaled deeply, exhaling slowly, enjoying the exhilarating pleasure that permeated his lungs. Eying his lieutenant, he spoke, "Pascano, it's obvious that Butler is not going to sell an interest in the mine; I offered him twenty million for a twenty-five percent interest; I thought he would jump at that price, but no, he would barely talk about it. What would you suggest we do?"

Pascano as the chief enforcer for the mob in that area; riding herd on bookies, shaking down local merchants for "protection", fencing all manner of illegal goods and even punishing wayward underlings. Yes, Pascano was a tuffy, qualified, according to him, for any job!

"Sir, I could take three or four men down there and put a hurting on Butler and his crew; that is, sneak in and sabotage his equipment, maybe break some knees to boot. You know, the usual thing!"

"Pascano, you amaze me, you recently told me that our contact at the airport warned about two guards, how they were marine snipers during the war. Also, didn't he tell you that all the people were carrying Schmeissers, even the woman? No, my son, this is a job for professionals."

"Now, I'm going to set up a meeting with the Director of International Solutions. They are a covert group, made up of former OSS (Office of Strategic Service) people that operated in France during the war. Their job was assisting downed flyers to get back to England or helping French underground. If they will take the job, I want you to go with them, just to point out the mine's location and the roads and general area leading to the mine. Understand that after you and your contact there have shown the location from the air, you return; I don't want you to get involved, in anyway with ground operations. Pascano nodded, but underneath, he was seething; well, if his boss had no more confidence in him than this, hell!, he thought to himself, I'm perfectly capable of accompanying these people when they start ground operations!

Late June weather turned blistery hot, even up the pass. Keeper had to seek shade as he left his quarters during daylight hours. Despite the heat however, his summer quarters here were easy pickings for him. His main fare, grouse and squirrels paraded near the boulders, within easy striking range.

The Owl brothers, Phillip and Henry, were training Buck to be a tracking dog. Buck would spend several days at the time with the two and he was elated when these sessions occurred. Now, he wouldn't be lying underfoot when Betty was busy with furbishing the Norton house, or making a nuisance of himself when George and I were working with the cave entrance.

During the meeting with International Solutions, Carlucci had outlined a plan to sabotage the Butler mine. No one was to be killed or physically harmed, only the equipment sabotaged. To this, the Director objected, "But what about my men, suppose they have to protect themselves, in case they're fired upon?" "That's their problem, like I said, don't harm anyone." Carlucci emphasized. "I don't like this, but I'll take the job, only under the condition that if this situation becomes too dangerous, we will discontinue it. Do you agree?" The Director was firm. "Fair enough," Carlucci nodded.

Piedmont flight 321 headed toward Charlotte, NC; left New York at seven am, aboard were Mario Pascano and Agent #1 of International Solutions, Inc. After a brief stopover in Charlotte, their destination was Asheville-Fletcher. During the flight, Pascano had attempted to draw his companion out in a conversation, but the man was non-committal. Never the less, Pascano wondered what kind of man would his boss pick instead of him, to do the coming job. He felt frustrated.

At the Asheville – Fletcher terminal, they were met by Pascano's contact from Sylva, and flown to the small landing strip there. Elevations from Asheville to Sylva varied from three thousand feet to five thousand in places, forcing the pilot to fly above six thousand feet for safety. The four-place plane had no heat and the flight was bumpy and chilly.

At Sylva, they were served a box lunch and coffee, while a mechanic serviced the plane. Once again they were in the air, this time, headed for the mine. Pascano sat in front, directing the pilot, by now, he was fairly familiar with the area, having spent two hours over the property earlier. For the next two hours, they flew back and forth, from every direction, while Agent One took pictures. When satisfied the Agent indicated it was time to go. At Sylva, the plane was fueled and the men flew to Asheville – Fletcher, where they took a seven o'clock flight back to New York.

At the time of Pascano's flight, the Owl brothers were in the woods, training Buck. They had heard the plane, but figured it was just another newspaper reporter, for the property had been constantly plagued with small planes flying over, or reporters showing up, wanting to take pictures. George and I were working at the cave and with the compressor and the air chiseler going, we failed to hear the plane over our own noise.

Back in Wilmington, Fred Barnes had finally hired a forester from International Paper Company. The man came highly recommended by the Marshall Brothers since they had purchased timber from that company. The timber had been cruised by the forester and the Marshall's had been satisfied with the results. Now, Fred could devote full time towards marketing our own product. Rachel was especially elated; each time she and Fred went to New York, she would spend the day shopping, while Fred conferred with prospective customers. Un-be-knowing, however, they were constantly monitored by Pascano and his cohorts.

During the first week in July, at around sundown, a car bearing North Carolina license plates, stopped on state highway #107; the spot had evidently been pre-selected. Hot, sultry weather prevailed, for savage thunderstorms had racked the area during the afternoon.

A man emerged from the vehicle and shouldering a backpack, he took a compass bearing and entered the woods. The car then sped off toward Sylva. The man's object was the road that led up the mountain to the mine. It was five miles away, through woods and sapling-strewn fields, forcing the man to constantly check his direction with the compass. With a tiny flashlight, Agent One could read right down to one degree on the compass, for he had to come out at least a half mile above the Owl Brothers trailer, just in case they had a watch dog around.

In Agent One's pack was an oxygen tank connected to an acetylene tank. In less than a minute of burn time, a one-inch steel cable could be severed by these tanks. Also in the pack with various and sundry small items, was a quart of whiskey, to be consumed after the man's objective was accomplished.

His eyes, now grown accustomed to the pitch-black darkness, Agent One pushed steadily forward. Caution was his first order, for there were limbs or small animal holes to be avoided. Some one and half hours later, he came out on the mountain road and was forced to rest a few minutes. While waiting, he listened for any foreign sounds, but heard none.

Now, on the open road, he could make better time and thirty minutes later came up to the cable car. Again, listening for any human sound, could hear none.

Locating the switch for the cable system, he started the cable car towards the mine, letting it run for three or four minutes before stopping it. Then lighting the acetylene torch, he cut the two main overhead cables. As the second cable parted, he heard a crash in the distance, as the cable car rolled down the mountain. Now, be could hear faint barking some two miles below, figuring the guard dogs had also heard the crashing. Now, it was time to take a hasty exit from the area.

Finding the well-trodden path that led upward to the beginning of the pass, he climbed steadily and reached the top in less than thirty minutes. Ah! Some rest and reward was well deserved, he figured. Finding a flat rock to sit on, he opened the pack and pulled out his reward, the quart of whiskey. Taking a deep draught and sloshing around in his mouth, he slowly let it sink down, enjoying it's soothing contents. For a long time he rested and drank, until half the bottle was consumed.

There was yet a long way to go. Plans were to go down the pass and follow the new cart trail and then the Norton road to highway #107. There, he would hide in the woods, near the Norton road, where Agent Two would pick him up on the morrow. If he were to reach this point before daylight, he had better get started!

Once again on his feet, but not so steady as before, he stashed the half-empty bottle and started down the pass. Sometimes, going down the mountain can be more precarious than climbing, and at times, he would stumble and fall.

Suddenly, Keeper was aroused by thumping noises coming down the trail; angered by the arousal, he lifted his head and waited. As Agent One reached the narrow path at the boulders, he lost his footing and fell against the rock. As the man struggled to regain his feet, Keeper struck, hitting the man's right side, under the shoulder. An immense does of venom, injected deep in the man's body, caused him to scream out in agony. Gaining his feet, Agent One lurched forward, the pain now causing him to go into shock. Struggling to keep moving, he fell again, crashing his face against a rock; he lay stunned for some time, before passing out.

Two days layer, Agent One was found by the Owl Brothers. They had discovered the damaged cable system and with Buck scenting the faint trail, had led them down the pass to the discovery. Even before reaching the scene however, they had spotted vultures ahead and knew that something was amiss.

The body was a horrible mess, hardly recognizable. The Owl Brothers notified the county sheriff and the state police. The body had to be sent to the State Coroner's office in Raleigh.

Agent One was an honorably discharged veteran of WWII; he had chosen a life afterward however, knowing it's inherent danger, it was his own choosing. Often times, it's not the foreseen dangers that do you in, it's the seemingly innocent, and that gets you!

George and I were discussing the situation about the dead saboteur, "What do you think happened to him?", I asked. "Well, the report from Raleigh stated that he had a high blood alcohol ratio and also a lethal dose of toxic venom. Either the concussion or venom probably would have been final; question is, which was first?"

George continued, "Although the body was badly swollen and picked over by vultures they were able to get some prints and dental record. He was identified as a former OSS man, of WWII." "In that case, I think I know who must have hired him; we can probably look for some more of this." I concluded.

Back in New York, The Director of International Solutions sat across the desk from Frank Carlucci; he was incensed, as he pounded the desk, "I've lost a good man," he shouted; "We simply can't operate with kid gloves. We are used to taking people from a distance." "Well, apparently, your man was so drunk that he fell and had a concussion." Carlucci laughed. "He tore up their equipment; has Butler responded to your offer?" Director asked. "No, you've got to keep on." Carlucci urged. "Very well, I'll make one more attempt, but it will cost you." Director shrugged. "Well, it looks like you're gonna have to tighten the screws, do something more drastic." Carlucci was empathetic "Such as?" Director asked, "Maybe cripple the guards, burn their house." Carlucci suggested. "Alright, one more try." Director said.

Phillip and Henry patrolled the entire pass, twice a week. Each Monday and Friday, they would drive to the Norton house ands start from there. Usually they let Buck go along to sniff for any foreign signs. On those days, George and I would not be working at the cave. Buck was becoming very proficient with his new profession, for it was he that had led the Owl Brothers to the dead saboteur.

A full month passed on the mountain, and nothing out of the ordinary occurred. Towards the end of August, signs of an early fall were evident, here and there. Under story dogwoods and sourwoods were showing tinges of red; above, yellow poplars began to shed a few golden leaves. Along the roadsides and fields, hosts of golden rods, asters, or thistles, invited their usual guests of bees and butterflies to dine. Yes, there was a certain crispness in the air.

Approaching dark, late one afternoon, a car stopped on highway #107 at the Norton road entrance. Two men emerged, each laden with heavy packs and also scope-sighted rifles. As their car sped away, the men turned and began walking up the Norton road. With a seven-mile trek in front of them, they hoped to reach the Camp Overhang in time to get some sleep before reaching their destination, very early next morning.

Caution was utmost and although both were well schooled, still they knew the Butler's had a dog at the house that could possibly give their presence away. Crossing the bridge, they proceeded on and found the trail that led to the Overhang. Once on the trail, they walked ever so softly, especially when they passed above the house. Safely out of hearing, they then stepped up their pace and reached the Overhang. Here, they made camp for the night.

At day break next morning, the two men broke camp and proceeded towards the pass. Once the pass was reached, they crossed the stream and started the climb on the Galloway tract. Reaching an elevation that allowed them to view most of the pass below, a favorable spot offered an opportunity to observe without being seen from below.

It being Monday, they expected the first Owl Brother to appear in the pass around nine am, the other brother would follow some forty-five minutes later. All this according to the contact at the Sylva airport. Their plan was for one of the men to fall in behind the first brother and trail him to a point where a favorable shot could be made. A shot that would be made to the man's leg.

As the two men waited and watched, the sun slowly crept into the pass, it reminded them of their days in France. Thirty minutes passed and Phillip Owl appeared below; his pace was unhurried, even deliberate as if he were searching for something.

The shooter was given the signal to move in well behind Phillip, all the time being careful not to be seen.

Five minutes and the shooter was down on the pass trail, but now his target was out of sight. Knowing that he had less than forty minutes now until the second brother would appear behind him, the shooter hurried up the pass. Presently, he caught a glimpse of his target ahead, but unfortunately for him, Owl had reached the boulders and had skirted them. Owl continued the slow pace, pausing frequently. Now, shooter had reached the boulders and rested his gun against it' side. There! Owl stopped, shooter found a leg in his scope and slowly began tightening the trigger. As he was squeezing the trigger, a terrific pain shot through his lower leg, the rifle slid and the shot went wild, narrowly missing Phillip.

Phillip plunged toward the ground, at the same time he heard the screaming from below. Cautiously, he raised his head and spotted the man, floundering around, screaming. Seeing the man had no weapon, Phillip ran towards him and reaching him, saw the man clutching his leg. "You sorry bastard, you tried to shoot me," Phillip yelled.

At once Phillip could see that the man was snake bit, he whipped out his knife and cut the man's pants leg off. The wound was in the calf, so he wrapped his belt tightly above it. The pitiful moaning continued. "This is going to hurt," Phillip said, as he began to make cuts on each puncture wound. He then began squeezing all the bloody poison from around the wound that he could.

Henry and I had been in the yard, talking when we heard the shot; fearing the worse, we jumped in the cart and sped toward the Overhang. The roads had been extended past the Overhang to the bottom of the pass, so it was only ten minutes until we were on the scene. While Phillip worked on the man, he explained what had happened.

The leg was beginning to swell horribly; we three picked the man up and began carrying him down the pass. Struggling and panting, the cart was reached in ten minutes.

How that golf cart held four men, I'll never know, but it got us to the Norton house. We called the sheriff to bring an ambulance. Later the man was flown to Duke.

Through powerful binoculars, the spotter, above the pass, had witnessed his partner's unfortunate event. He had correctly guessed that the man had been snake bit, an instant before the gun was fired. What was amazing though, was when the man that was fired upon, came to his partner and proceeded to administer aid. Then shortly two more men arrived and helped carry his partner down the mountain. He reasoned then, that all of them were trying to save his counterpart. "Hell, if we're trying to harm these law-abiding people, then why am I being involved with this mess?" After the group had left from below, the spotter made his way back to highway #107, where he would hide until his men would pick him up.

September continued to get cooler; it was now time for Keeper to leave the Pass and seek food down below. He would make daily searches, leaving the cave early and return late in the afternoon.

George and I worked at the cave and now the opening was almost large enough for a man to enter. We wanted it much larger, in case a hasty retreat was necessary. At the beginning of each workday, George would play a ten-minute tune at the cave's entrance. This was to let Keeper know that we were friends. The soft violin tunes seemed to mesmerize the snake.

Two weeks after the snake-bitten man was transported to Duke, details finally reached the Director of International Solutions. The man had lost his leg, but was recovering otherwise. Not only was he singing to the North Carolina State Bureau of Investigation, but the FBI, as well! Naturally the Director was somewhat embarrassed when the FBI confronted him, but after all, his organization was a quasi-government concern, and nothing would come of it. Director confronted Frank Carlucci and bluntly told him that the deal they made was finished. Naturally, Carlucci was disappointed and angry, but the FBI was now close to the scene, but decided it best to not pursue any further prospects. Perhaps in time, another opportunity would present itself! Pascano had kept abreast of events, for why not? He had made many trips to Wilmington spying on Fred Barnes and several trips to Jackson County. He was aware of how much the Butler emeralds had brought during the early summer auction in New York. Was not Fred Barnes also a member of the Butler Company? With all those millions floating around, surely there must be an opportunity for Pascano to get a piece of the pie!

Early Tuesday morning, September 20th, George and I loaded the golf cart with supplies and headed for the cave. We figured to work longer than usual, hoping to finish the cave's entrance. A cloudless blue-sky overhead, coupled with a palate crammed with fall colors on the mountainside, filled us with excitement. Perhaps we were near the end to find out what the cave would reveal, after eons of hiding its' secrets! Above the gentle chug of the cat's motor, we could hear Tommy Holden's two bulldozers working to the east, on the Galloway tract. It's surprising how far sound will carry on a crisp morning!

Unloading the equipment near the cave, George took up his violin and played some soothing tunes, next to the opening. If Keeper was inside, this would soften his anxieties brought on by the noise of the air chisel we would be using.

Now, the opening was at least six feet high and two feet wide, but we would be working on the sides. It should be three feet wide we had agreed.

Steadily, working until noon, we took a long break for lunch. Holding a thirty-pound air chisel below your waist-level isn't so bad, but as the height increased, you are forced to rest more often. Consequently, we had to frequently spell each other.

Resting for some forty-five minutes after lunch, we again began to attack the opening. Our ears were ringing with the deafening clack, clack of the air chisel and we failed to detect the three masked men who had crept up behind us. I was on the air chisel, when George suddenly tapped me on the shoulder; surprised, I looked around and stared into the muzzles of three Thompson sub-machine guns.

"Shut the motor off," one man yelled, at George; "now, you two get away from that opening." I wondered who these masked men were and what they wanted; I was to find out shortly. "Well, well, so what do we have here," apparently the leader asked. "So, there must be something valuable in there; perhaps emeralds?" Had I heard that voice before? Was it at the banquet, given by Auctioneers International?

"Say, whose violin's that?", the leader asked, as he pointed to it. "It's mine", George replied. "Well, old man, if it's yours, why don't you step up and play us a tune, let's say something like Beethoven", the man cackled in a high pitched laugh. Now, I was sure, I knew who the man was; it must be Pascano, connected to Frank Carlucci.

George picked up his violin and took up a position just outside the cave's entrance. Lifting the instrument, he began to play, but it wasn't what I expected to hear. What came out of that instrument was the most God-awful sound that you could possibly imagine! It sounded like Satan was on a rampage! The sounds drifted inside the cave; they struck the forked tongue, the musical vibrations entered the pits, near the eyes of the Keeper. He was shocked, enraged Moving from the rear of the cave, he took up a position near the cave's entrance.

"Stop that screeching nonsense", Pascano shouted at George, as he grabbed a flashlight and strode toward the cave's opening. "Now, you two, guard these clowns," he ordered his men, "I'm going to see what's in that cave."

All of us were quiet, waiting expectantly to see what would happen to Pascano, as he disappeared into the cave.

Even with the flashlight, Pascano was at first partially blinded from stepping from bright daylight, then into pitched darkness. He focused the light ahead of him, then to the ceiling. There, glittering by the dozen, were ends of emeralds, reflecting their dazzling green. Pascano gaped, wide mouth at the sight. Continuing transfixed, Pascano failed to see the great triangular head that rose by his right side. With open mouth, it struck him in the neck, one fang piercing an artery, the other entering his windpipe. The man pushed the great head away and emitted a scream that died in a gurgle. He turned and staggered towards the opening.

Already, in a few short seconds, the massive dose of venom was reaching Pascano's brain, he was becoming disoriented and beginning to lose consciousness. Plunging through the cave's opening, face down and emitting croaks and gurgles, his eyes rolling around, Pascano was dead in less than two minutes!

At the sight of their boss plunging through the opening, the two guards rushed past, completely ignoring us, momentarily, it was then that George and I jumped them, from behind, quickly disarming the two.

Waving the Thompson at the two, I said, He's dead, there is nothing you can do for him, now; let's get him loaded on the cart. Take off your masks.", as I ripped the one off Pascano. "I want to know his name and yours." At first the two were silent, staring sullenly, towards the ground. "Very well, George, go cut me a long Spruce pole; since they won't answer me, we're going to lash them to a pole and push them into the cave." As George picked ip an axe, the two men screamed at once, "No, please", at that they named Pascano and jabbered each of their names.

It was impossible for the cart to hold four men and a corpse. We lashed Pascano's body in front with me and the two men sat in back, facing the rear. George walked closely behind, the Thompson sub-machine gun pointed on the prisoners.

The grind down the mountain was slow, arduous, with Pascanos' corpse continually butting against me. Also, it was difficult for George, since he had to keep one eye on the ground and the other focused on the prisoners; this, while carrying a heavy machine gun. When we had reached the halfway mark at the beginning of the white oak ridge, I insisted that George and I change places, figuring that riding was easier than walking. After all, George was almost twice my age! The trip down took the better part of an hour; for the cart could go no faster than the man walking behind.

Finally reaching the Norton house, I was in for a shock; Betty came running out of the house, crying. "Rachel has been kidnapped; Fred just got off the line and he is hysterical." "Well, where is he?" I asked. "He is in New York and right now with the Finklesteins. While he was conducting business with them, Rachel went shopping and didn't return to the hotel, and then, Fred found the kidnapper's note on his door." The note said they wanted a million dollars, or Rachel would never be seen again." "When did this happen?" I asked. "Sometime yesterday; Fred was with the Finklestein's all day and got back to the hotel late that afternoon."

I thought for a minute or so, then concluded, it must be the mafia people, Frank Carlucci or Pascano. They were the only ones that I had contact with at the banquet; that is – people who would do such a thing. Well, there was one way to find out and it was right in front of me.

Turning to the two prisoners in the cart, I asked them a simple question. "Gentlemen, how would you two like to go back up the mountain and spend eternity in that cave? If you don't tell me the God's honest truth, we are going to take you back up the mountain, lash you to a long pole and push you into that cave. You can see what happened to Pascano, here. I am going to ask you this – did you two help Pascano kidnap a woman, a Mrs. Barnes, yesterday." I turned to George, "George go call Henry and Phillip and tell the to get here at once." George started for the phone in the house, when the two started screaming, "No, no, please. Yes, we helped Pascano take the woman, he threatened us if we wouldn't."

"Hold up, George," I called, "they helped Pascano." I told Betty to get Fred on the phone and in two minutes, she brought the long extension to the door. "He's on," she said.

"Fred? This is Bob, now, listen up, I'm going to put a man on this line and you write down his directions, make him repeat the directions. Now, next thing, ask the Finklestein's if there is a Mossad near that they can quickly get in touch with. Now, here is the man, listen carefully."

I drove the cart near the door and handed the near man the phone, taking it, he began talking to Fred, "We have your wife in a small town of Blacksburg, right across the line in New Jersey. Here is the location and telephone number. Now, I will call the guard and tell him there has been a mistake and for him to release the woman to your people when they come." The prisoner then hung up and dialed another number, speaking loudly, he instructed the listener to release the woman unharmed when the law or others came for her. In ten minutes, Betty got Fred back on the phone and handed it to me, "Yes, Aaron contacted the Mossad and they are on their way, now." Fred was overjoyed and kept thanking me, over and over.

While we were waiting for the sheriff to show up, Betty, feeling sorry for the prisoners, brought them some food and soft drinks. Late that night, Fred called and thanked me several times. Rachel was with him. Fred said the Mossad (Institute for Intelligence and Special Operations) quickly located Rachel and returned her to the hotel.

Throughout the course of one week, Frank Carlucci was visited by the Federal Bureau of Investigation, The Mossad, the North Carolina Bureau of Investigation and the New York State Police. "All this was brought on me by that idiot, Pascano". Nothing was proved yet, of any connections between Carlucci and International Solutions, however, the FBI was still interested.

For the past two weeks, we had been operating the mine and processing its' contents for the coming auction in November. Fred had been on top of the market and thought we should enter only a modest amount of emeralds. After all, we were highly successful in the spring auction, so it really didn't matter to me. After all, it was the market that determined the mine's output.

October 20th, a special day for Betty, George and I. A day that we had set aside for a particular occasion! Today, we planned to enter the cave!

The morning broke bright and clear, blue smoke curled lazily skyward, frost on the pumpkins, as the old saying goes, produced millions of diamonds, or sapphires – even rubies and emeralds, at the whim of the rising sun.

Betty was busy in the kitchen, she had fired up the big kitchen range and the aroma of burning oak and hickory wood whetted one's appetite. Anticipations soared, with the thoughts of crisp-oven baked biscuits, scrambled eggs and bacon, all washed down with freshly brewed coffee. The last tomatoes from the garden, that she had picked yesterday, not only decorated the plate, but better yet – flavored the other ingredients.

Shortly, I heard a door slam outside and George was knocking on the door. We sat down to a sumptuous breakfast – the old fashioned kind, produced by that big wood range! Buck was even alert, it seems that the smell of food will bring him to full attention, even from the deepest of sleep!

While Betty fixed a lunch, George and I packed a few items in the cart. Several flashlights, burlap bags, a small box; items that we thought might be handy, if we found something in the cave.

With Betty and Buck in the back, George cradling his violin, sat in front with me. Off we started up the mountain, jumping several deer, every few minutes. As we approached the long white oak ridge, a large herd of wild hogs scattered in all directions. Grouse, turkeys and squirrels were everywhere here; the acorn crop was prodigious this year.

Stopping near the cave, we carried the equipment the rest of the short distance. The cave appeared dark, somber as we approached. Confident that Keeper was inside, for he did not emerge very early on cold mornings, George said, "You two stand back and I will see what happens. When I call out, you can also enter, bring your flashlights." With that, he lifted his violin and strode to the cave's entrance. Shortly, he began to play, not the rasping devil's tantrum that had contributed to Pascano's end, but long soft tones; soothing to any soul!

Keeper rose from slumber, from the back of the cave, lifting his head

137

some three feet off the floor, he swayed from side to side, mesmerized by the music and seemingly keeping time with it.

George advanced slowly, now well inside the cave, he called for us to enter and to train our lights toward the cave's rear. What an awesome sight – the giant triangular head swaying from side to side. George continued to play, but slowly, slowly reducing the sound. Finally Keeper turned and disappeared into the inner cave. "It is safe now." George uttered, softly.

As we played out lights all around, the scene was fantastic, almost like being in a dream. Large clay pots lined both walls, Betty walked over and shining her light, let out a loud gasp, "They're full of all kinds of stuff, arrow points, pipes, spear heads, stone axes. We went from pot to pot and it was the same for each one. From the ceiling, there sparkled the ends of emeralds that were embedded!

We selected an array of items for our own pleasure. "George, after we have examined all these pots, I want to dedicate most of this stuff to the Cherokee Museum." I said. "That would be a great idea; these things would certainly add to the history of my people." George was elated. For the better part of an hour, we examined the pots and their contents. Finally satisfied, we stepped out of the dark cave, into fresh sunlight; almost as if we were emerging from a dream! Deep in our thoughts, still awe struck with what we had witnessed.

Keeper would not be disturbed, he would be allowed to remain in his domain, to roam free, wherever he chose!

George gazed up at the blue sky, "It's about time for hunting season to roll around." I nodded, "Yeah, it's been a long time between hunts." Maybe at last we had found peace and quiet.

BIOGRAPHY

Robert Edney, a retired forester, has worked for some forty years in six southeastern states. Buying land and timber, selling real estate, managing thousands of acres of timberlands and procuring thousands of cords of wood to feed paper mills.

Some of his most exciting periods of work have been in the Cape Fear lowlands of North Carolina, the Santee River swamps of South Carolina, the Savannah River and Altamaha River lowlands in Georgia.

Encounters with rattlesnakes, cottonmouths, alligators, wild hogs, moon shiners or irate landowners were a routine occurrence.

After four years of service in World War II, Edney enrolled in the University of Tennessee and later transferred to the University of Georgia, receiving both a BFF and MF in Forestry.

Edney's hobbies are hunting, carving, golf and researching forest products. Managing his forest lands takes up a great deal of time.

SYNOPSIS

Following the close of Word War II, Robert Butler returns to the United States. He and his wife Betty are determined to pursue a long cherished dream; that dream is to move to a beautiful, sparsely settled section in mountainous North Carolina. An area filled with mountains, rivers, waterfalls and vast stretches of forestlands. Robert's exposure to the teeming millions of people in India and China during the war, makes him more determined than ever to find an area with few people, where he can live a life of peace and quiet.

Loading their few belongings in a surplus army Jeep, Betty and Bob, along with Buck, their big Airedale, set out for western North Carolina.

The search ends in Jackson County, a beautiful mountainous county. Here they are able to buy a large mountainous tract of land that has an old farmhouse and a high mountain peak. At first, they are forced to struggle to make a living, but then their discovery of what the mountain reveals, profoundly changes their life, from anything but peaceful to one of immense danger and excitement. As one continues fully into the story, the excitement that unfolds is enough to spur the reader to pursue it to the end.

Breinigsville, PA USA
18 November 2010
249493BV00001B/2/P